Trespassers Caught

Maud and Emma Investigate

ANNA CATMAN

For book orders, email orders@traffordpublishing.com.sg

Most Trafford Singapore titles are also available at major online book retailers.

Printed in Singapore.

ISBN: 978-1-4669-3210-4 (sc)
ISBN: 978-1-4669-3212-8 (hc)
ISBN: 978-1-4669-3211-1 (e)

Trafford rev. 05/22/2013

 www.traffordpublishing.com.sg

Singapore
toll-free: 800 101 2656 (Singapore)
Fax: 800 101 2656 (Singapore)

Contents

Accessories and text attribution

'I've just found an extraordinary thing,' Emma told Maud when she called her up on a Sunday afternoon.

'What is it?'

'A novel, in a bag,' Emma said.

'In a bag? Where?' Maud sounded less surprised than Emma wanted her to be.

'You won't believe it. At a bags show. I've been to a craft bags show this afternoon. You know, these shows where people who sew and knit bags or craft them out of leather exhibit. I love things like that, you know. I've even tried my hand at making bags myself. And there I've found a bag. And most surprisingly of all, there is a novel inside!'

'What do you mean you've found a bag?' Maud said, after a pause. 'You mean you've stolen an exhibit?'

'No, of course not,' Emma said. 'How can you think it? This bag was a separately standing bag, all by itself. Somebody must've put it on the floor, just for a few seconds, and then moved on and forgotten.'

Emma sounded quite convincing and, indeed, what was impossible about it? But somehow Maud felt that there was something slightly unnatural about this story, but she couldn't put her finger on what it was. She herself never found a bag, separately

1

standing or not, with something in it, but maybe other people did? She couldn't think about anything else to ask Maud about the bag. In fact, they weren't her kind of thing at all, she wasn't in the least interested in them and even considered belittling for a woman to be so.

'What's the novel about?' said Maud.

'Oh, the novel . . .' Emma was hesitant. 'It's . . . lovely. What do you think it is about? Try to guess.'

'I don't know. Love? Passion?'

'No-oo.' Emma sounded disappointed now. 'Of course, not. Do you think I would be so excited about it if it was a love and passion novel? How boring and unoriginal. You've got two more attempts left.'

'Ok,' Maud said. 'Maybe middle life crisis?'

'Slightly warmer,' Emma said. 'But just slightly. It's kind of painful, at least, at times, to read about your own preoccupations. But you are right that this would interest me more than a love and passion novel. Are they not the same thing, on the other hand, only too often? Only one go left for you now. Try hard.'

'It's about . . . About . . .' Maud stumbled. 'I don't know. I give up. What else can a novel be about? It's about vampires making up their home on an UFO and setting up a new legislation for settlement boundaries?'

'It still reminds me of something,' Emma said. 'Doesn't it to you? But it's a good try, I admit it. If you were playing darts, you'd get the first circle from the centre if not the centre itself. Yes, it's on immigration.'

'Oh,' Maud said. 'You are hopelessly social-minded. On immigration? Do you really think it's a better topic for a novel than love?'

'I don't know if it is, but it's the one I like more,' Emma answered.

'So, what it's like?' Maud asked, again. 'You should bring it in at once. I'm dying to see it. By the way, why didn't you take it to the lost property at the exhibition?'

'Oh, come on,' Emma said. 'We can always do it later, let's have a good read of it first.'

When Emma came, Maud immediately grabbed the bag with her two hands.

'Oh,' she said. 'It's a Luis Vuitton bag, isn't it? Is there a logo? Do you think it's real?'

'No, I don't think so,' Emma answered.

'So it's a fake Vuitton bag you've found. How can you be so sure?'

'Look, the trademark sign is not at all where it should have been normally,' Emma said. 'And anyway, wherever it is, you can see it's part of a picture. The front panel of this bag is decorated with a picture of a woman who holds a bag, big for her size, and the label is sewn onto it. It's just a picture of a woman with a Luis Vuitton bag. I think it's absurd to ask if her bag is real. So you see,' she concluded, 'it can't even be counted as a real fake.'

'I wouldn't be so sure,' Maud said. 'Of course, it's a trademark on her bag, the woman's in the picture, but it's also on yours. Your bag is in the real world, and because it is, this sign is forgery.'

'Mmm,' Emma said. 'Yeah, I guess you can say this Vuitton sign staples two worlds together. Or two bags—the one in the picture and the one I'm holding. But after all, it's not even meant to look like a real thing, I'm sure. Somebody just embroidered it here because . . . because . . . because they felt like it.'

'Show me what's inside,' Maud said. Emma opened the bag and took the pile of printed pages out.

'It's a manuscript,' she said. 'Of a very interesting novel. Look.'

Maud pulled out one page of a stack and read:

'It is twenty years today since the day when I arrived to my new land by ship. This ship was full of people who like me had chosen to change their fate from outside rather than inside by changing the circumstances of their life. Most were looking for a better life and some wanted to find a new identity. I suppose I can safely say that more often than not they found something other than what they were looking for. Those looking for a new identity for themselves most often were the ones who found a better luck, and those looking for a better luck changed themselves in the process so much that hardly anybody from their previous life would recognize them. But however much I've changed since the time when I got off this ship, twenty years ago, I've always found it difficult to share my insights in the process with my new compatriots. Whenever I was starkly sincere, or should I say, unnecessarily explicit, I was almost invariably suspected of withholding the truth and even lying. On the other hand, if I managed to remember that a lie could be more convincing to some people than truths that they found improbable, on the basis of their own experience, so different from mine, I was able to pull my story through quite successfully.'

'How sad. He sounds like a lonely guy, doesn't he? It's a bit like a letter in a bottle. Have you ever felt this way yourself?'

'Yes, many times,' Emma answered. 'I'm a migrant too, remember? But didn't you? By the way, why do you think the author is him? There is no name on the title page. What if it's a woman?'

'I don't know.'

'It feels to me like it's written by a man, but, on the other hand, some women do write like men. And vice versa. Not too many, though.' Emma said.

'What do you want to do with it now?' asked Maud.

'I don't know,' Emma said. 'I haven't thought about it. We can always take it to the lost property, it's never too late to do it. I want to read it all first. It resonates with me so much, you know. Actually, I'd like to take it to an editor somewhere and see what happens. And wouldn't the author himself, whoever it could be, like it? Especially if we can pull it through. Let's try.'

'He may even thank you later,' Maud said.

The friends have chosen next Monday two days later for taking the manuscript to publishers.

4

'What are you going to say there?' Maud asked Emma. 'You must have a story to go with the novel. You can, of course, tell them that you've found it in a fake Luis Vuitton bag which is not really a fake bag because the trademark sign is a picture of a sign, not a sign, but I doubt it will help you.'

'What does it matter where I've found it,' Emma said. 'A text, you said once yourself, remember, has a life of its own. It is independent of its creator. And even more so, I suppose, from the circumstances of its discovery.'

'Well, it may be true,' Maud said, 'but it's usually said in a different context. About people who are dead already and have been for a long time. Are you sure your author is dead?'

'No,' Emma said. 'How would I know? And if anything, I kind of feel, that the author is alive. I have a connection, you know.'

'Well,' Maud said, 'If you are looking for a story, he better be dead. Then this bag story starts looking even romantic. Although if he is indeed dead, there must have been a third party who put his manuscript in the bag you've found. Unless he did it himself and died immediately after.'

'He doesn't sound like a suicidal type from what I've read,' Emma said. 'Do you mean to say that, if the author is dead, his life circumstances are not anymore important?'

'Nobody's really, in my view,' Maud said. 'It's just that the other day I read somewhere that Pushkin—or was it Byron?—anyway, one of these great poets was deeply in debt and constantly juggling many loans, and how awful, from this writer's, who lives some two hundred years later in a different part of the World point of view, this must have been. And I thought that after all these years the person who wrote it must be the only one who is still interested in the subject of this debt. But what it does demonstrate, is that . . .' Maud stopped, trying to formulate her thought . . . 'It does show that the author's life circumstances surrounding, so to speak, a certain literary project, do matter to some people. And even surprisingly so. And even many years later some people find it relevant what may not be relevant to you. So my point is—think your story through carefully, before you make the first move.'

'Well, you can't blame people it they want to know who was the beauty for whom a certain poem is written, can you?' Emma said. 'On the other hand, if you like the lyrics, what's the difference, who was it written for, and what did she look like? Although I don't quite feel this way, I admit. But I see your point. I think I'll make up a few stories at once. And we'll try them all. The only problem is I've never tried this sort of thing before. So I suppose I must rehearse my part beforehand.'

When they approached the first publisher's office Emma said to Maud:

'Let's tell them the story I've told you, just once. And see what happens.'

'No,' Maud said. 'This won't work.'

'Then let's not say anything at all on this subject. We'll tell them I want to publish it, and that's it. Let me handle any questions.'

In the office they were greeted by a secretary and led to the editor's office through a short corridor. A brown-haired woman, tall and slim, apparently in her early fifties, was standing near the wall. Her looks vaguely reminded Emma somebody she knew long time ago. Or did she really? She knew that sometimes déjà vu can be unjustified but tried to remember where she might have seen her. The woman looked at her and smiled. She flicked through the pages Emma handed her and looked out of the window.

'You lure people,' she suddenly told Emma.

'I beg you pardon?' Emma said. She should have been taken aback, but she felt so surprised that she didn't manage to express any emotion.

'You lure men in your nets,' The tall slim woman repeated.

'What men? What nets?' Emma asked. 'Why do you say this? And how can one lure an adult person anywhere anyway? What do you mean? Who?'

'It's obvious from the kind of bag you are holding, 'the woman explained her thought. 'I can just feel it. You lure.'

'No,' Emma protested. 'How would you know? Have you met me before? Do you follow me on the sly? I'm not doing this kind of thing, and I'm afraid I won't be able to explain to you why. And anyway, even if I was, what does it matter?' She paused for a second, and sighed deeply, looking around trying to find good arguments.

'It's not my bag. I've found it at a show,' she added.

The tall slim woman took a minute to answer why it does matter, and all the time Emma was looking at her through a blur caused by her explosion. She thought strange and unnecessary thoughts. One of them was, perhaps, less fuzzy than all the other, most of which Emma wouldn't be able to dress in words, even if somebody asked her. The most clear of her thoughts was: is this woman married? Does she have children? The answer seemed obvious to her: no, of course, not. 'But why am I so sure?' she asked herself. But she was sure. The slim woman still didn't answer her questions. She looked at the pages and maybe even tried to gather her thoughts. And meanwhile Emma went on with hers: as surely as I know that this woman who I see for the first time in my life never had children, she knows when she looks at me . . . What does she know? Emma couldn't quite guess what the woman knew, but knew she did know something, not quite obvious to Emma.

'I told you, you must have a story. You can't just load off a pile of printed pages on her desk,' Maud told Emma, once they stepped out into the street.

'Not with her, anyway,' Emma agreed. 'But you know, the most interesting thing in this encounter is that this lady seems to be convinced that the owner of the bag I'm carrying must be a great seductress. Why, I wonder? It's not even a real Vuitton. And it's not mine, remember,' she added.

'What's a great seductress, anyway?' asked Maud. 'Doesn't it sound medieval? Do people still get seduced? Who? where?'

'I guess it depends on who you are dealing with? Don't you agree?'

'Some people may be significantly more strict about these matters than other,' said Maud. 'They think it makes them better and derive personal confidence from being chaste. I heard some such folk with my own ears. On the other hand, one can derive as much confidence and self-assertiveness from being tolerant and open to all kinds of experience.'

'Do you necessarily have to practice it?' asked Emma. 'Because I don't want to. In theory, I'm with those open to everything guys. But in real life . . . I don't know . . . I have other things on my mind . . .'

'But you carry a bag that suggests the opposite,' said Maud. 'Why?'

'I don't know,' Emma replied. 'Does everything have to be internally consistent? Anyway, it doesn't suggest anything of the kind to me. Perhaps I just live in another what do you call it? Space? In that space it was considered a bad taste to start a discussion of personal matters unless you were very clearly invited.'

'This first attempt didn't work because of you damned bag. I suggest you get rid of it and try another story,' Maud said after a pause.

The next day Emma turned up at the Union Square, the friends' meeting point, with a big pink office folder which she carried in a transparent plastic bag.

'Is this bag any better?' Emma asked Maud.

'What's your story today?' Maud said. 'Have you thought of anything at all?'

'I don't know,' Emma mumbled. 'I suppose I should choose somebody I knew well enough as the author of the manuscript. Maybe my father?'

'Was he a writer?'

'Well, in a sense,' Emma sounded pensive and uncertain. 'He was a scientist actually, a chemist, and he wrote some poetry as well. Many people do at some points of their life.'

'But he lived in another country, didn't he? What are you going to do about it?'

'I don't know. I suppose I could say this stuff is a translation. It's hard to prove the opposite and nobody would bother anyway. Even to try, you've got to be able to read in both languages.'

'Both what?' Maud asked.

'Both his original stuff and this one I've got in the folder,' Emma said.

'This is not going to happen, you are right,' Maud agreed. 'When did he die, by the way?' she asked.

'A while ago,' Emma answered. 'I think it's been fifteen years now.'

'Does this stuff you are so keen about feels like very . . . you know . . . contemporary thing? Tied to the moment?'

'Not really. Not to me, anyway. But it's situated in a place where he's never been. Don't you think it's an obstacle?'

'Not really,' Maud said. 'Why would that be? He could have imagined things. If this kind of things mattered to him, of course. But it's not the sort of detail anybody would go into. You just have to be consistent on time and place when your manuscript has been written. If you do, it will come off all right. Whoever you'll say did it, the important thing is the name should be a respectable one.'

'Do you think I should anglicize the name?' Emma asked.

'I'm not sure,' Maud replied. 'Sometimes authenticity, even a fake one, sells better.'

Without having decided anything on this important subject, they knocked on the door. They've been led into a small room where a slightly fat slightly balding man with an unpleasant, to Emma's eye, expression in his piercing blue eyes offered them two seats.

'Well?' he said.

'I have an enormously interesting manuscript to offer,' Emma said. 'It's been written by my father before his death fifteen years ago.'

'Who?' the balding man asked.

'My father,' Emma repeated. 'He was an acknowledged writer in his own country, you see,' she said. Actually, she lied here a little, but she felt this bit was the most important one to be established in the little man's head.

'Yes,' she said and breathed deeply. 'It's a very interesting novel on women-migrants' inner conflicts and, you know, settlement stories.'

The little balding man looked weirdly at her. He could have asked if her father was a woman-migrant and whether he was very prone to contemplating inner conflict in himself and others. He could have asked this and perhaps some other questions, but he didn't, and Emma with an insight that she herself appreciated as rare, thought that this was probably the most remarkable thing about the present conversation. And maybe even something worth appropriating.

'Ok,' the fat man said. 'Leave it. I'll look through it, but I can't promise anything, you see.'

'Do you think he meant he'll do it?' Emma asked Maud when they closed the door behind them.

'What do you think?' Maud said. 'The important thing is, he was civil. And not too particular about your accessories, you know. I can see you've got a new mother-of-pearl pendant today,' she said and went on 'I've told you, it's a good story in your situation. And if you ask me, he hardly knows himself what he means. It's just a wrong kind of question.'

'You know,' Emma told Maud a few days later, when they were still waiting for a reply of a piercing blue eyes man. 'I'm feeling a bit tired of all this now. Let's try something completely different now. What if we go out there and tell them it's me who's written this novel?'

'What?' Maud said. 'Is this true? Why didn't you tell me this straight away?'

'I don't know. Maybe I was timid, you know. And I certainly wanted to see what's your impression is going to be, if you don't know who's written it.'

'You've liked it, obviously,' Emma said. 'Or you wouldn't be going with me to all these places, would you?'

'Of course, you can say that. But if you think closely about it, you'll see that there are two different explanations possible. I'm with you in this business of door-knocking because I've really liked your novel. Or it could be because I'm a true friend of yours.'

'Or it could be both, couldn't it?' said Emma. 'I'd like it to be both. Are these two things independent of each other, you think?'

'Yes,' Maud nodded, rather solemnly. 'By the way,' she said, still looking sinister, 'the reverse it true, too.'

'The reverse? What reverse?' Emma asked.

'If somebody doesn't want to help you or have anything at all to do with it, it can be for the same two reasons: they either don't like your novel or they don't like you nor want to be your friend. One thing entails the other. It is actually the same thing for many people. Do you still want to try again?'

'How can they not like me if they don't know me? And why? What have I done?'

'You can't know what they know,' Maud disagreed. 'Well informed people know everything they may need to. Do you still want to try?'

'Yes. I want to see at a close range how it works. And why. I may even come out of this a better person, right?' she added.

The next publishing person Maud and Emma visited was a man in his thirties, of unremarkable, as Maud put it to herself, appearance. He looked through the manuscript. 'I take it English is your second language, is it not? Why did you choose to write a novel in it, then?' he asked Emma.

'You see . . .' Emma was trying to be as accurate as possible. 'I've been living here for a long time now. Sometimes you can speak of a certain, you know, reality, only in the language you use to live in it. Another language just wouldn't fit. Sometimes you can't even find the words you need in it.'

The man was looking at her, but nothing in his appearance seemed to suggest that he understands, or thinks it is a good reason. Emma tried a more sociable explanation.

'I wanted people I see every day to be able to read it. Like, you know, you start imagining what this and that person would think when they read it. Most people I see every day don't read my first language.'

Something must have clicked when she uttered her last words. 'But to me, it's a kind of trespassing. You can't write a novel in your second language. It's unthinkable,' the man said.

'Some people did,' Emma protested. 'And anyway, what do you mean, calling it trespassing? Is your language a kind of private property?'

The man didn't say anything, but Emma did. 'You give me an idea. I know what name I should publish it under now. It's going to be 'Trespassers W.' Or does William Trespassers sound better, what do you think, Maud?'

You may not believe it, but just a short time after 'Inner conflict in women-migrants by William E. Trespassers' has come out in hard cover.

Codebreaker's cupboard

'Did you know I've started a new job recently?' Emma told Maud one day.

'Really?' Maud sounded surprised. 'I had no idea you were looking for one. What is it?'

'It's in the library,' Emma said. 'I guess you can say I'm a junior librarian. You know I like books. And I don't have to get up too early for that one either.' When Maud congratulated her on this achievement, Emma continued. 'You wouldn't imagine what I've found the other day in the back room.'

'What?' Maud asked.

'A big wooden cupboard with quite a few drawers, full of handwritten filing cards. You know, the kind of cards they used to write catalogues on before it was all replaced by computers.'

'But it's no use to you now,' Maud said. 'Don't you have a computerised catalogue and readers' access system?'

'Sure we do,' Emma said. 'But what's in the cupboard is not a catalogue.'

'It's not?' Maud showed some signs of interest, at last. 'What is it then?'

'That's the problem,' Emma said. 'I don't know. You see, part of this stuff is written in a code, and I can't read it.'

'A code?'

'Yes,' Emma nodded.

'What does it look like?'

'I guess it must be a fairly common type,' Emma said. 'It's numerical.'

'What's a numerical code?' Maud asked. 'Does it have something to do with numbers?'

'Yes, of course. It's a code in which each letter of the alphabet is replaced by a number. All drawers of my mystery cupboard have inscriptions in this code. Little paper notes stuck to the front of them.'

'Why do you think it is a code?' Maud asked. 'Maybe they are numbers, after all,' she added hopefully.

'I don't think so,' Emma said. 'The numbers on the drawers have nothing to do with what's inside them. The top drawer, for example, has number 142 stuck on it. What would you expect this number to be? Naturally, the number of cards in the drawer. But it's not. There is only one hundred cards inside. So you see, it can't be the number, it's the code.'

'It doesn't have to be, from what I've heard so far,' Maud observed. 'What if somebody has just removed the other forty two cards? Even if there were more cards in the drawer, it's not conclusive. They may have added the cards, but didn't change the sticker.'

'But there are number stickers on the other drawers too,' Emma said. 'And they are, most of them, four digit numbers. Do you think there could have been that many cards in the drawer? It's a small library.'

'How do I know?' Maud said. 'What's on the cards, anyway?'

'The cards are . . . They are . . .' It looked like Emma wasn't quite sure how to explain it, 'They are on people. Presumably, people who used to come there to borrow books. It's what you'd call their personal information.'

'How long ago would you say it's been written?' Maud asked.

'A while ago, I think,' Emma answered. 'I'd say, at least ten years back. The cards are all yellow and old now.'

'It's strange they haven't destroyed it, isn't it?' Maud said. 'Given that it's old and of no use now.'

'Well, I think, it's not, really,' Emma said. 'If it was up to me, I wouldn't destroy it, either. Especially, before I crack the code and can tell what it all means. Besides, not too many people use the room. At the moment, it's all mine.'

'Whose room was it before you started there?'

'I'm not sure, actually,' said Emma. 'But I guess, I can find out, just by asking people at work. I think, it was the person's who did the same thing I'm doing now.'

'Which is?' Maud asked.

'Maintaining the catalogue,' Emma said. 'If you come there, say, tomorrow, after we close at eight, I'll show it all to you.'

When Maud came to see Emma at the library the next day, the automatic door was already close, and she had to ring the bell. It was summer and the light outside was just beginning to fade. The outlines of all the objects in the library seemed slightly hazy to Maud who could hardly breathe normal after her fast walk. 'It does look mysterious in this light,' she thought. A moment later Emma turned the switch on and the fluorescent light from the ceiling flooded the rooms.

'Are you sure it's a good idea?' Maud said. 'Anybody could know we are here with the light on.'

'It's alright,' Emma said. 'We won't be able to read otherwise. I often stay on later after work. Come on, I'll show you the cupboard.'

They entered what was, evidently, Emma's office and Maud was struck by the huge size and appearance of the cupboard she's come to see. Its surfaces were polished to the point of shiny and of such a deep black colour she rarely saw in wood.

'What is it made of?' Maud asked Emma, trying one of the smooth surfaces by touch.

'I don't know,' Emma said. 'I guess it's wood. Somebody must have brought it from home. It seems unlikely that it was bought as one of the library furniture items. Come here, I'll show you the code.'

Maud came close enough to be able to read the yellow stickers on the cupboard's drawers. There were just five, in fact. The top one simply read: 142. Next to the number, there was a picture of a man made of stick legs and arms, with a rather imperfect circle for a head.

'So?' Maud said. 'Why do you think it's a code? Can't it just mean that there are 142 cards inside? Or there were? What's on the cards, anyway?'

'Let's see,' Emma said. She opened the drawer and showed Maud one of the cards. It read:

'Meagan Smith. 37. 15 Greenwich crescent, married, two children. Romance, crime, true crime.'

'Well, this is not in code, is it?' Maud observed. 'And it does seem pretty straightforward, doesn't it? It's just readers' names and addresses. They always take these. As for those 'crime' and 'romance' words, they must be her reading interests. Perhaps they took note of these to be able to offer her something she'd be interested in. You know, if they'd get a new Romance book for their collection, they'd mention it to people who like this kind of books. I see no mystery there'.

'They took some information on families, too,' Emma said. 'Look, for this lady, for example, they put down that she has two children.'

'It can be for the same reason,' Maud said. 'To be able to offer her something she'd be interested in borrowing. Children's books, I mean. And nothing indicates there is a code here.'

'Look,' Emma pointed at the stickers on the two drawers underneath the top one. The first one of them read 6448, and the second 3449. 'Do you think these huge numbers have something to do with what's inside?' she asked.

'I don't know,' Maud said. 'Are they so huge? How many cards are there?'

Emma pulled out the second drawer from the top which had 6448 on it. There were just a few dozen cards inside.

'It can't be the number of cards here, I see,' Maud agreed. 'But maybe, just maybe, this number stands for something else? How many books they borrowed all together, for example?'

'Who would need to know this?' Emma said. 'And if they did, they'd probably note, then, what it is. It's not the number the meaning of which you can guess naturally. But wait. I kind of just realized what proves it's a code. See this number 'four'. It's repeated in all three stickers: the first one is 142, the second 6449 and the third's 3449. It's also on the bottom two ones. It would be strange if these were just numbers, don't you think? I think it's a letter, most likely a frequent one. Something like 'e' or 'o'.

'Oh,' Maud said, impressed. 'Well, it does sound convincing. But there are just a few words here. It may not be easy to work out what they mean.'

'Yea—h,' Emma agreed, but sounded hesitant. 'We can have versions, you know.'

'Versions?' Maud repeated. 'Do you have any yet? Which one is more frequent, anyway, 'e' or 'o'?

'E' is, but sometimes you can take one for another,' Emma answered. 'Many words end in 'e' and very few ones do in 'o'. One of my favourite ones is 'bravado'. Usually this is how you can tell . . . But we don't have any stickers ending in '4' here,' she added.

'Let's write it down, if we want to think about what it means,' Maud said and pulled a page out of the notebook. She wrote what the five stickers on the drawer read in a column:

142
6448
3449
348
150348

'The last one is really a huge number,' Emma pointed out again. 'It can't possibly mean the number of anything that's inside'.

'If it is a numerical code where a number stands for each letter of a Roman alphabet,' Maud said 'it will contain two-digits numbers, obviously. And there will be a problem of breaking it into letters. You see this last sticker starts with 15. It can be either fifteen or one and five.'

'And what if they used the numbers bigger than twenty six?' Emma said. 'Just for fun, you know. I'm terrified already.'

'Let's start with 4,' Maud said. 'Let's write down what we get in both cases: when 4 is 'o' and when it is 'e'. There shouldn't be too many possibilities'. She wrote on her piece of paper opposite the column of numbers:

	Version one	Version two
142	1O7	1e7
6448	6OO8	6ee7
3449	3OO8	3ee8
348	3O8	3e8
150348	15O3O8	15e3e8

'Look,' Maud said. 'The first word is, obviously, a short three-letter word with an 'o' or an 'e' in the middle. Like lot or got, or set, or get. There are loads of them.'

'Most end in 't','Emma said. 'So we can be fairly sure that 2 stands for a 't'. But the next two . . . can be anything, I guess.'

'Even if we accept it that the first drawer contains the information on all the readers the person who wrote it dealt with, there still seems a lot of possibilities. It could be 'lot' or 'got' or 'set'. And even 'get'.

'Why do you think she's drawn a man next to it?' Emma asked. 'Is it part of the code?'

'It could be,' Maud said. 'But I don't think so. It's quite clear that it is a numerical code. Maybe she—how do you know it was she?' Maud interrupted herself.

'Only women work here,' Emma said. 'So?'

'Maybe she was thinking of something. Other codes. Remember dancing men?'

'Look, the last two words are part of each other,' Emma said. '348 and 150348. I think it stands for 'men' and 'women'. It seems natural these words are there if somebody has been taking, you know, demographic information. Then 8 is an 'n', 4 is definitely an 'e' and 3 is m. 15 must be 'w',' she added.

'Great,' Maud continued. 'Then we can read that 3449 word too. If 3 is m, it starts with 'mee'. Must be meet.'

'But remember, we decided that 2 must be 't',' Emma reminded. 'Because it's a three letter short word like 'set' or 'got'.'

'I think it's clear now that 't' is 9,' Maud said. 'How else you can read that thing that starts with 'mee'? Ok, let's leave it at that. We can always return to what that last sticker means, later. Anyway, I think it's quite clear now: the first drawer contains the information on everybody who has been using the library, and that one with 3449 sticker on it—on people she actually met.'

'What if the sticker says 'seen' not 'meet,' Emma said. 'Let's look, what's in the drawer,' she added. 'We hardly have so far.'

Maud took one card out of the drawer.

'I met J. today for the first time. He is a tall, good looking man with short whiskers. His conversation is not very interesting for me and is mostly centred around his job. His reading interests seem to reflect this. He borrows, most often, 'instant success' and self-help books,' she read.

'Well,' Emma said. 'I think I kind of know how she saw people. But why did she do it? Try another card.'

Maud took another card from the drawer.

'N's life, if I may say so, revolves around love. She is what one would call a perfect romantic heroine. But of what time? None of the periods I know of would fit her: her changes in mood and attraction are too sudden, and the reasons and circumstances that prompt them are rarely discernible to anybody but her. She reads mostly gardening books,' it read.

'Not bad, eh?' Emma said. 'I knew somebody like her, by the way. I think, the person who wrote it, was looking for somebody. Or something.'

'Maybe some connection between what people read and what kind of people they are?' Maud suggested. 'It's the two kinds of information she always noted. But why?'

'I don't know if I can answer this,' Emma said. 'It's kind of self-explanatory, don't you think. I mean, it would be interesting to find out what the connection is, if there is one, wouldn't it?'

'Of course, there is one,' Maud agreed. 'There is, probably, even two. It's a two-way road: a person's character matters, of course, for what they read, but also what they read may influence what people are like.'

'There should be some limitations on this obvious statement,' Emma said. 'If you read about vampires, does it make you want to suck blood? And it can be, of course, that it's mostly aliens at heart like to read about aliens, but I don't believe it.'

'Fair enough,' Maud agreed. 'I think there are some areas, if you like, where this connection works.'

'What areas?' Emma said.

'You see, I think there is one area in everyday life where we are mostly influenced by books.'

'Which one?' Emma asked.

'Which one? Don't you know?' Maud asked. 'It's romantic love, of course. If we couldn't read about these things at all, your attitude to these things would be quite different.'

'So?' Emma said.

'I think,' Maud continued 'your woman was looking for some kind of connection between what people read and what kind of love they can experience. Or the other way round: how their domestic life reflects what they read.'

'I heard something like this before,' Emma said. 'It's been done before.'

'So what?' Maud said. 'It only makes it more likely. She might have heard about it too, and decided to try it herself.'

'Possibly,' Emma said. 'But you know, these cards, they don't sound like research to me at all, if you see what I mean. It's more like a diary. And why did she use the code?'

'I think it's obvious,' Maud said. 'She wouldn't be allowed to take these notes if somebody knew what they are for. She would need to disclose her goal and get a permission. If she didn't want to, as I suppose she didn't, she had to cover up the whole process somehow. So she used the stickers on the drawers. As for the cards themselves, as you say, they may be taken for the diary entries.'

'There are no dates on them,' Emma said. 'And although all names are abbreviated with just one letter, the addresses are full. Anybody can read them, as well as the content of the card.'

'Perhaps she knew that nobody was going to be too inquisitive, if it wouldn't be too obvious, what it's for,' Maud said. 'And it's not obvious. The kind of 'person-to-a-type-of-book' thinking I'm suggesting is just a guess. For me, it's the easiest, but it may not be the most plausible one. Have you read all the cards, by the way?'

'Not yet,' Emma said.

A few days later Emma called Maud again.

'You won't believe it what I've found!' she said.

'What?' Maud asked through a yawn. It was still early morning.

'There are coded cards in the drawer!' Emma said. 'I've found two! These must be most important ones and a clue to the whole affair. Come at once, I'll show you.'

'I can't come right now,' Maud said. 'I have to be at work.'

'Ok, I'll see you in the evening, eight o'clock as before,' Emma said and hung up.

When Maud was approaching the library door in the evening, she felt a small shiver of uncertainty and expectation running down her spine. What can be in these coded cards? Was Emma able to read it by herself now? What if they've run into some kind of important and sinister secret here?

'An important secret like what?' she asked herself. She tried to remember what other codes she heard of were used for, but couldn't.

'Show me the cards,' she told Emma as soon as she was inside the library building.

'Look at this one first,' Emma said, taking a card out of the drawer. 'It's not that hard to read it, actually. It's got lots of letters we already know. Look.' The card read:

314 155892 90 3049 321 93146. 154 35344 5 34594.

'Look,' Emma said again. 'There are plenty of 'e's here and some other letters from the stickers we read last time.'

'Is 4 an 'e'?' Maud asked. 'I remember it is. Look, this word after the dot has 15 in it. Unless it's 1 and 5, it must be 'w'—we know it from that 'women' sticker on top of the top drawer. So the first word in the second sentence is 'we'. 'The next word,' Emma said, 'starts with '3'—it's an 'm'—and ends, again, in 4. It must be 'made'!'

'Can't it be something else?' Maud said.

'It can,' Emma said. 'Make, mane, mate, mare and male. But it's unlikely. I think it's 'made'. And then we know what numbers 'd' and 'a' are, and you see, the next word starts with 'da'.'

'Is 'd' a double digit number?' Maud asked.

'Yes, it is,' said Emma. 'It's 34. Remember, we knew from the beginning that it can be. So, I say, the next word starts with 'da' and ends in 'te'. It's a 'date'. We made a date,' she read from the card, very happy to have made it.

'She wrote here that she made a date with somebody. But why?'

'Maybe it has something to do with the rest of the cards?' Maud said. 'What does the first part of this coded card say? Let's work it out and maybe we'll see. We know what numbers stand for 'a' and 'e', and some other letters. Let's write down those letters we know for the first part of her message.'

Emma wrote something on a piece of paper and showed it to Maud. It looked like this:

X e XXXXXwed mXtXXeX.

'I've used crosses instead of all letters we don't know,' Emma said.

'I think that first word must be 'he,' Maud said. 'What else can it be, if she was going to a date?'

'It could be 'w,' Emma said, 'but we know it's not 'w'. So it's 'he' all right. He did something. What?'

'I think he borrowed,' Maud said. 'The number of letters is just right and it ends in 'wed'. Besides, what else can you do at a library?'

'What did he borrow?' Emma said.

'Is it important?' said Maud.

'I think it is. This was the kind of information she noted for everybody. But it's obviously in the last word. What can it be?'

'M . . . starts with an 'M,' Maud was looking for a word, but couldn't find it.

'Mitchell!' cried Emma. 'He borrowed Mitchell. We made a date.'

She read it all, radiant and happy. 'What does it mean?' she asked. 'Why did she write it in a code?'

'I think she wrote it in code,' Maud said 'because it was important. And maybe she wanted to hide the fact that she made a date with a reader because she wasn't supposed to do so?'

'There is nothing wrong with it,' Emma said. 'It's perfectly allowed. But I think there was something else in it. She was looking for something, perhaps, trying to hide the process of her search. What do you think she was looking for?'

'I think it's obvious,' Maud said. 'She was searching for a perfect partner. But in some peculiar way . . . I'm not sure what exactly was her plan . . . But I think she believed, maybe, that what people borrow sheds some light on how they would behave in love. Or can it be that she was trying to influence their conscience through books?'

'Let's read the other note,' Emma said. 'What does it say? I think we know enough letters now to make it easy.' She took the other note out of the drawer, leaned over it and after a minute's contemplation, read:

'He borrowed Jane Eyre. I think he is the one.'

'I think you are right,' Emma told Maud. 'She was looking for somebody she could love among people who came to borrow books. And it mattered to her what they read—otherwise she wouldn't take notes of it.'

'Do you think she found him?' Emma asked.

'How would I know?' said Maud. 'I wonder if there is a way to find it out, I mean, for us,' she said, pensively.

'If it was, after all, one of these two guys on the cards,' Emma said 'it shouldn't be too difficult. Look, there are their addresses here, and they are not even in code. We could go and see them, if they still live there, of course.'

'Do you think she married one of these two?' Maud asked.

'I don't know,' Emma said. 'I'd like to know. I can see what it was like for her now,' she added. 'What book do you think the person she found perfect would read? I mean, all in all? Perfect not at just one passing stage of her life, but, you know, forever?'

'What if,' said Maud, looking at the stickers again, '4' stands for 'o' not for 'e?' 'Instead of 'meet' this could be 'room,' she said, pointing at the third sticker from the top.

'Yeah, but the coded cards wouldn't be readable then,' Emma said. 'What do you think is the first word, the one on the top drawer? I mean 142? We only know it's got 'e' in the middle, but neither '1' nor '2' have occurred so far.—No, wait,' she added. 'We know that 2 is 's'. So it's something ends in 's'. What? I don't know any such words. I mean, three letter ones. Apart from 'yes'. Can it be 'yes' on the drawer?'

'A bit of this sticker has been torn off,'Maud observed, pointing at its uneven right edge. 'There were another letter or two here. Maybe 'best'? What can it mean?'

'Maybe, she took notes not on everybody she met at the library, but just on some people?' Emma suggested. 'Those she found best in some respect? But which? What was the feature she assessed? What could it be?'

'My guess would be,' Maud said, 'that 'best' were those people who were most interesting from her point of view. They must have been all males, if she was looking for a partner.'

'But it is not so,' Emma said. 'There is about the same proportion of men and women in her cards. This explanation won't do unless she considered female partners too. I guess it wasn't all that simply utilitarian.'

'Maybe she noted those people who reacted to what they read in a way she liked?' Maud said. 'But how would she know?'

'She talked to them,' Emma said.'I think we should find those people on her coded cards and see. Maybe we'll understand better what she wanted then.'

When a couple of days later Maud and Emma set out to meet the two people on the coded cards, they were suddenly intercepted by an ordinary-looking dark-spectacled man.

'Hello, ladies,' he said. 'I'm sure you are looking for me.'

'Who are you?' Maud asked.

'I'm the person you are looking for. The one she found perfect.'

'How do you know we are looking for you?' Emma asked, too.

'Oh,' he sounded puzzled by the question. 'I don't know how, really. Just felt something strange, I guess. It happens, you know.'

'What's your favourite book?' Emma asked. 'Are you one of these two people on the coded cards?'

'No, I'm not,' he said. 'As for the favourite book . . . I'm not sure I should tell you, actually . . . I'll think about it and maybe will come and tell you later. Goodbye for now.'

'This was strange, wasn't it?' Maud said.

'Why?' said Emma. 'I don't think so.'

What was it?

Emma got off the train and went into the underway near the railway station. She wanted to buy some ribbons in her favourite shop. As she stepped into the underway something caught her eye in the gutter. She leaned down and picked it up: it was a small postcard. She got out of the underway and sat down on a bench to have a better look. The card was a picture of a girl. She reminded Emma of somebody, but who? She tried to pull the person out of her memory, but couldn't. 'Maybe later,' she sighed. 'I can have another good look at it, when I get home.' She turned the card over and almost gasped: something was written on it. She couldn't tell why, but somehow she didn't expect it. On the other hand, she told herself, if she was sure that nothing at all was written on it, why had she picked it up. She couldn't even remember what side was up, when it lied in the gutter. It read 'Elder Bovar'. There was a phone number, too. 'It looks like a mobile,' Emma thought. She looked at the numbers again. The first two were 04—all mobiles started like this. The next one was 1980—the year she was born in. The next one was 10—the day when she was born, and the last one was 08 which was her street number. All digits, it seemed, apart from the first two, had something to do with her. Could it be a coincidence? Emma was sure it was impossible. There were too many of them—those which were in some way her numbers. But how did it happen? Could it

27

be that somebody can actually choose mobile numbers? Pick up the digits and their order? Or maybe, it wasn't a real mobile number at all? There was only one way to make sure—to call it—but somehow she felt she doesn't want to do it. But what was she going to do with it? Throw it away right now? She sighed and put the card in the pocket of her bag. 'I can always decide later,' Emma thought and went inside the shop.

She was walking along shelves of multicoloured thread and needles of various sizes, trying to decide what cloth to buy for new curtains. Suddenly she remembered that it happened a few times before that she found things that seemed to say something to her. In fact, it happened all the time. She stopped near a packet of glittering letter stickers hanging from a hook. There was a pair of scissors next to the letter W. 'It looks like somebody is trying to tell me something,' Emma said to herself. 'Like you are going to cut up your happy life—W—if you keep the card.' She made a few more steps along the shelf. A big smiling sticker of a face hung next to a sew-on heart pattern. 'It means something like that too,' she thought. 'Is the card the same thing?' she asked herself. 'I know nobody is actually trying to speak to me here, through the things on the shelf. It's just a certain way of looking at them. If you look at them in a certain way, you see messages. It's madness, actually, because there are no messages. Nobody wanted to say anything. Just piles. Is the card the same?' She walked on and tried to think hard. 'How can I be sure? Because I know that nobody knows I'm here. But how do I know it? Couldn't just about anybody see me in the street? Or see me with a camera? Doesn't it mean that whatever strange arrangements I see now on the shelves could be, just could be, intended for my eyes?' She stopped and was looking now at the counter where a girl cut the cloth for customers. 'But I know it isn't true, anyway,' she concluded. 'Nobody came in here and moved the letter stickers for me to read. It couldn't be. But what about the card?' She started walking toward the shop exit. 'I wonder if there are any cameras in the underway near the station,' she thought. 'I'm sure I was alone there when I picked up the card. It's naïve,' she decided 'to think that you can go anywhere these days without being noticed. If this is so, everything could be there especially for her—the card with the strange number, the seemingly talking configurations of things on the shelves. Crazy,' Emma sighed. 'Knowing that nothing goes unnoticed makes you crazy.' There is no difference between a piece of paper that somebody might have put there and then because he knew she would be there in a few minutes and just everything else. But somehow she knew nobody played with the stickers on the shelves for her, but the card, she felt, was meant for her. Was it really? Was it a love letter?

Outside she deeply breathed in and felt better. She didn't know, although often wondered, what parts of the street, if any, are surveyed, but always felt better outside.

While Emma was waiting for the train at the station, she found herself next to a guy engaged in a mobile conversation. She couldn't help but listen. 'Man, I'm stuck here,' the guy was saying. 'There's been no train for thirty minutes and you know what I feel like. I just want to go to Southland to hang out for a bit. You know, man, just to walk around. But there's been no train for ages.' Something was said on the other side, and the guy went 'I can't afford to repair my car, man. I haven't got a job right now, man. Mum wouldn't let me to use hers. Jenny? Yeah, she's got hers.' The person on the other side said something again, and the guy said 'No, man. I've just applied last week. You know what they said? They said my resume is too long. The man there, he said, man, he said my resume is three pages long, but it should be two, damn it. I said, it looks cool this way, man, but he just wouldn't listen. I'll tell him again, man. What d'you reckon?'

Emma felt compelled to turn her head and look at the person whose life was too long and complicated to fit into the space allocated for a resume. The man was about twenty five, white, despite his constant 'man-man' refrain, and pleasant looking. There was something peculiar about him and almost recognizable, but again, she couldn't tell what it was. His interlocutor said something. 'You don't get it, man. I'm not having any alcohol yet. I'm just feeling better now,' he answered.

He waited, listening for what the other person was saying, and repeated. 'No. Not yet. I'm just feeling better.' 'Do you think I should make my resume shorter, man?' he added after a pause.

'I'm feeling better, too,' Emma thought. 'Especially when I come here to get ribbons and stuff. Could it be, him, maybe,' she thought 'who dropped the card? We seem to have so much in common. But I don't know him and it looks like whoever's written what's on the card did know a lot about me. No.' The guy must have felt something because he's finished his mobile conversation and started talking to Emma. 'Awful, isn't it,' he said. 'I've been here for thirty five minutes. Maybe even longer.' Emma nodded and said 'Yeah.' He went on. 'When I was a child, they always did something with the line. I mean, there were railway works, you know. All the time. But there are none whatsoever now, and I think all the problems are because of this. You gotta make an effort, you know. Maintenance is the thing.' He looked at her expectantly, perhaps waiting that she'd tell something about the railway of her childhood, too. And maybe other experiences. While she was trying to decide whether it will or will not be completely out of place, the train came, and she got on it. The guy did so too, but they didn't talk anymore. The card in the pocket of her bag bothered Emma, but she thought it's best not to look at it on the train. She could always do so later.

When Emma came home, she drank a cup of tea and ate a sandwich. All the time she remembered the card, and it seemed to her that when she'd be looking at it here, at home, everything will become clear at once. She took the card out of her bag and looked again. 'Strange,' she started where she's stopped before, 'the girl on the card reminds me of somebody. But who?' She brought the card closer to her eyes to look at the embroidery on the girl's dress. It was cross-stitched. 'Cross-stitches mean something,' Emma thought. 'Does it mean she's bearing a cross? But why? When, by the way, was the last time I've seen cross-stitches? Certainly not in this part of the world,' she decided. 'Strange,' she went on 'that I should pick up a card with an embroidered dress in it near a sewing shop. Who could know I'd be there? That's the question,' she concluded. 'Where did they print the card?' she asked herself. 'And who are they? How many people do I know who can actually do it? Not too many, maybe, but not too few.' She made herself another cup of tea and turned the card over to look at the other side again. Again the combination of numbers she read struck her as something unbelievable. Next to the numbers she read a few words. Or were they just letters? In fact, she read them when she first picked up a card, but only now noticed what it was. 'Lemma' was the first one. 'What a strange word,' Emma mumbled. 'It has something to do with maths. Quite a rare word. My name is Emma. It looks like it's meant, indeed, for me. A message. Is it genuine, I wonder?' Two other words followed lemma: 'case lap'. Does it have something to do with computers? But they were laptops, not laps, right? She couldn't tell what it means, but felt the meaning was somewhere close. How could it happen, anyway, that the person who wrote the card, whoever it was, left it here? The card with her name? Lemma, she was sure, had something to do with her, couldn't be otherwise. If the person who wrote the card meant that it should be her who'd notice and pick it up, he must have known that she was coming there. But how? And who was it? She had no idea, or did she?

She waited a minute and started all over. The day was Thursday, and since she was paid in the morning of this day, she would often come to buy things at that shop and later would have a cup of coffee nearby. Often, but not always, however. Could one just count on that and it will turn out to predict it all right? 'Maybe,' she decided. 'But one doesn't need to rely on pure chance,' she suddenly realized. 'Train carriages definitely have cameras, it says so on the wall of every each one of them, and perhaps you could see where somebody gets off if you know how.' It seemed convincing. Her whereabouts were first predicted by somebody who knew what she was likely to do, and later, perhaps, just followed through. But who was it? She felt so drawn into the whole thing now, that her judgment, she slightly suspected, started to blur. All kinds of people seemed likely candidates to her. 'Am I just a bored and rather lonely person looking for ciphered letters right under my feet on the ground?' she asked herself. 'But the name on the card can't be accidental. It's really strange to pick up a name like this.'

'Something can be done,' Emma decided, 'to find out more. To investigate the card. It certainly is one of the strangest things I ever held in my hands.' The most obvious way to find out more, was of course, to ring the number. But somehow this was not what she wanted to do. She was convinced the number couldn't be real, and, on the other hand, if it was real, how can you call it when you have no idea who might answer? What if it is some kind of a trap? She'd call it, and somebody she knows and doesn't want to call will answer. What then? What would she say? What would she look like before everybody after she's made this call?

Having thought that, Emma decided to set a trap of her own. She could, of course, show the picture to just about everybody she knew and ask questions, but this would be time and effort consuming, and people's reactions might be not as natural. They should just see it, unprepared. She decided to enlarge and frame the picture and to set it up on her desk in the library. Most of her friends and just accidental acquaintances such as readers would then see it. Somebody might betray himself. She wasn't sure what a person who'd betray himself would do, but was sure she'd recognize it.

Two weeks have gone by since Emma set up the cross-stitched dress girl's picture on her desk, but nobody seemed to have reacted in a way that would tell her something. 'Who is this?' most people asked. Emma explained that the picture was a portrait of her remote cousin that was e-mailed to her, which she'd set up on her desk because she especially liked it. It turned out convincing enough to most people, and nobody had shown any disbelief. 'On the other hand,' Emma realized 'if people don't ask who it is, they may be just indifferent or tactful. Not everybody wants to know.' She was still waiting for somebody whose reaction would be unusual enough to be counted as self-betrayal. But nothing like this happened. When the second week of her observations was drawing to a close, a tall and stout woman came to borrow books from her. Emma was sure she'd seen the woman a few times before, but didn't know her name. She looked at the picture, when she was about a step or two away from Emma, and was obviously taken aback. She looked scared. 'She's seen it. This is it,' thoughts rushed in Emma's head. 'She must be short-sighted, she's just noticed it,' she added as an afterthought. The lady's name was, as Emma found out using her card, Olga Wriggs. Like many, she asked Emma where she got the picture from, but her voice, Emma was sure, was trembling. Suddenly Emma told her a slightly different story. 'Just found in a magazine,' she said. 'Do you like it?' 'Yeah,' said the woman. She seemed in a hurry to take her books and go and did so.

'Well, it doesn't help much,' Emma thought. 'It looks like she'd seen it before. She didn't ask who it is. Just where I got it. And it wasn't just an empty question to her. But even if it is true and she'd seen it all right, what do I do with it now? And where did she see it? What if she'd seen it right here through the window when she was passing by in the street? Or on the library's camera?'

Her trap idea didn't seem to have yielded any results. 'What if people just react differently to it because they have, what do you call them, natural differences?' Emma thought. The answer, if she was to find an answer, lied somewhere else, but where? 'How much information can you squeeze from a general knowledge that quite a number of people may know where you are at any given time?' she asked herself. 'Not much, exactly because it's quite a number of people.' She recalled every detail of the card's layout but couldn't find anything that would be an obvious, doubtless clue. She rolled the words 'lemma case lap' in her mind again. What if the whole thing is an anagram?' she asked herself. The idea seemed promising to Emma and she started tossing the letters this way and that. At last she realized that there was one combination which seemed better than all the other: pale sac. But what does it mean? Sac, she knew, was 'a bag' in French, but still . . . It didn't make much sense. But what if they mean 'sea'? Pale sea? And even better, it was a name of a café not very far away that she knew quite well. 'Oof,' Emma breathed out, feeling that she really made some progress. If this is an invitation, there must be a time. What if the first 'l' in 'lemma' stands for . . . What can it stand for? One o'clock? Or was the time, if it was, indeed, the time, the number of 'l' in the alphabet? The day when she found the card was long gone, however, and the time, whatever it could be, didn't really matter. Missed it because she couldn't read the message! She felt really disappointed. Somehow the thrill of reading the hidden message on the card coloured her expectations of what she could find in the 'Pale sea' if she was there at the indicated time. What was it she could find? She had no idea. Even less than no idea because she didn't even know who was inviting her. But it didn't matter, she was really sorry she didn't come. 'Maybe it is not too late now?' thought Emma. 'What if I turn up there today? Perhaps I could expect to find the same person there. Or maybe not. We'll see.'

When Emma came to the 'Pale sea' that night she found her old friend Jack there. He looked surprised to see her and, she thought, perhaps calmly pleased. 'I'm here every night,' he told her. 'How have you been?' 'Was it him who wrote the card?' wondered Emma. Of course, it would be the most natural supposition under the circumstances, but somehow he seemed really surprised to see her. She remembered Olga Wriggs' reaction when she saw the card on Emma's desk. Olga, on the other hand, was not surprised to see it. Whatever her emotion was, it was not surprise. What should she make of it? Was Olga somehow involved in the whole business? How? Could she have written it?

'I should obtain a handwriting sample from both,' Emma decided. It seemed easy. She asked Jack to sign a birthday card for a common friend and with Olga it was even easier: she had to fill in a reader's information form. Finally, Emma could compare both samples with the card! It was Olga's handwriting that looked similar to the one on the card. 'Of course, it's not decisive,' Emma thought. 'To be sure, I must have asked for an expert's opinion. Actually, there may be too few characters on the card to say anything for sure.' Did she actually want to be sure? She didn't know it. Maybe not. If it was Olga who did it, why? Why did she want so much to organize a meeting between Emma and her old friend? She didn't even know Emma apart from short formal meetings in the library. What did she think when Emma put her borrowed books through? Did she like her? Or quite the opposite? Could you actually hatch a plot like that (Emma was sure it was a plot) because you like somebody? But why?

Thinking about unexpected turns of human character she looked at the three little sheets of paper before her. It was nearly dark in the room and the characters were no more discernible, but she kept looking.

The bloody scarf

'Not again,' Emma sighed, when she found out that trains had been cancelled and she'd have to wait for a bus. It was a cool Sunday morning. She came to the station to catch a train, only to find a small square around it full of people. A small crowd has split into groups, according to, roughly, age, sex and nationality. A group of Chinese girls was chirping near the kerb. A few middle-aged Indian ladies, wrapped in beautiful shiny fabric, embroidered in some places with beaded stars, stood a bit closer to the platform. One of them, who looked a bit heavier, than the other two, was sitting in a chair made of iron wire, one of the three there were. A blond young guy with a folder stood by himself, leaning on a tree. Two Greek women with huge cotton bags looked as if they had an innocent plan of spending this Sunday morning at the market.

Having taken in this scene and trying to estimate the waiting time as well as she could, Emma made her way straight to the second of three iron chairs behind the platform. For all she knew, it could be twenty or even twenty five minutes before the bus comes. She eyed the crowd again and wondered where all these people were going. Was it work? On a Sunday morning? She herself was going to work and didn't mind it, especially given that she didn't really have much choice, but who else could be like this? She tried to work out how many of these people could be going to work now. 'Some may just have a habit of getting up early,' she decided. Suddenly one more woman came and sat in the third of the three iron chairs. She was around sixty, overweight and looked a bit wobbly on her feet. She stumbled and nearly fell down, as she was approaching the chair, but straightened herself and finally didn't. The woman leaned her back against the chair. 'There was the same thing yesterday. It took me two hours to get to work,' she said. 'What do you do?' Emma asked. 'Pardon?' 'What do you do?' Emma repeated, wondering, if she should add 'for a living', but didn't. 'I'm a nurse,' said the woman. She sighed and half closed her eyes. It was obvious that she was extremely tired. 'I like your scarf,' Emma said. 'This one?' the woman picked up the black felt scarf with her hand. She had two around her neck. Another one was yellowish green in colour and looked much smoother. 'This one,' said the woman, 'was given to me as a birthday present just yesterday. Unusual, isn't it? It's hand-made felt. My birthday isn't coming until June, of course, but she thought of it now, and I do think it is very nice of her.' She paused and left Emma wondering what sort of reply could be expected of her in this situation. 'Why did she give you a birthday present now, then?' But it sounds kind of blunt, and almost impolite. Or, maybe, try 'Where did she buy this beautiful scarf?' The answer is obvious, at a market stall, but it does sound much better than the other question. Instead Emma looked around. 'I wonder, if I'm going to be late again,' she said. 'I don't mind it taking longer,' said the other woman, 'but the buses are so full. I can't stand it. There aren't enough buses, they should have more.' 'There are plenty,' Emma said. 'Only they come all at once. I wonder, why.' 'I don't mind, if it takes two hours,' the woman said, 'as long as it's safe.' 'I always get upset, if it takes longer,' Emma said. 'She must be living by herself. Otherwise . . . ', she thought of the woman, but before she could finish her thought, the woman stood up and walked fast to the nearby taxi stand. A second later she got into the taxi and drove off. Emma looked at the chair and gasped: the nurse had forgotten her scarf. The hand-made black one Emma admired. It was too late now to run after her, or make any signs and noises: the taxi was nowhere in sight. Emma picked up the scarf to touch it and have a better look at it and almost screamed: when she turned it over, there was, no mistake there, a big blood spot on it. Actually, two. Another one, a bit smaller, was perhaps, she decided, simply a trace of the bigger one, left by folding the scarf in the middle. Did the woman leave it here on purpose? Where was the blood coming from? Should she run and report it immediately? 'Calm down,' Emma tried to reason with herself. 'If she's a nurse, it probably means nothing. She cut herself and wiped the blood with her scarf. Or cut somebody she looks after.' It seemed the most plausible explanation. The only thing that troubled Emma a bit was that, as she imagined, nurses don't usually wipe blood with their clothes. If they did, that is, there'd always be blood spots on everything they wear. But there aren't, normally. Leaving a scarf on the chair made it suspicious. If the blood spot was an innocent accident, why was she trying to get rid of it? 'I'll find out,' Emma told herself and got on the bus that finally came. She folded the scarf in four and put it into her bag.

For a couple of days Emma thought mostly about the woman's scarf in her bag. 'I can always come to the station on Sunday morning, when she is there, and just follow her. That is, if I don't go to work myself,' she decided. This seemed simple enough, but, of course, could be noticeable. Was there any other way? She wasn't sure, but, unexpectedly for her, one day the woman came to the library, when Emma was working there. 'She may remember me,' Emma thought. 'And she certainly knew, who I was, when we first met. She probably wonders, what I've made of her scarf. I could tell her and see, what she says. Or, maybe better not to?' She hesitated a minute, and when the woman approached her desk, decided to speak up. 'Remember, we met last week,' Emma said. 'You know, when trains were cancelled. What's your name, by the way?' She didn't have to ask this question, in fact, because the woman was about to ask Emma to scan her card. 'Val,' she said. 'I remember you too. I've forgotten my scarf there, on the chair next to you. You haven't seen it, by any chance, have you?' 'A scarf?' Emma wasn't quite sure, what she was doing next, and tried to think fast. 'Yeah, I've seen a scarf. There was a blood spot in it. In fact, even two. So I threw it away right there. Was it yours? How did it happen?' 'One of my clients cut himself at breakfast,' the woman said. 'Remember, I've told you, I'm a nurse.' 'I don't have it anymore,' repeated Emma. 'What's your client's name? The one who cut himself?' It was, of course, a clumsy and brutal attempt, but it seemed at the moment like the only way to move forward with her investigation. 'I can't tell you, obviously,' said the woman. 'Why are you asking?' 'Why have you left it there, if you need it?' Emma asked. 'I didn't notice I left it behind,' said the woman. 'I've lost it, not left it there on purpose.' 'How strange people can be,' Emma thought. 'Did she change her mind? Or can what she says be true? Did she subconsciously decide to get rid of the evidence and later regretted it? Anyway, she must want this bloody black felt thing badly, to come here.'

The woman gave the three books she's chosen to Emma to scan, but instead of going away immediately after, sat down at the computer. 'She doesn't have one at home,' realized Emma. It was easy for her to pass behind the woman's back, when she was typing in her username and password. 'It'll give me a chance to learn a bit more about her,' thought Emma. 'What is she looking for on the internet, I wonder?' The woman, it turned out, looked for a winter jacket. She wanted it to be made of pure wool and dyed with a special kind of dye, called a natural dye. Right now she was trying to find out, moving from one link to another, what kind of dyes fall within the category of natural dyes, and where they were manufactured. Emma got so interested in dyes herself, that she almost forgot what was her purpose. 'If I look into her account, the first thing I should find out is whether any of her friends and acquaintances went missing or got murdered recently. Somebody could just be injured, maybe not even seriously, of course, but somehow it doesn't seem likely to me. I say, would she try to get rid of the scarf then?' Emma passed behind the woman's back a few more times and a new thought occurred to her. 'What about those people she works with, her clients, as she calls them? It's unlikely they send her e-mails, not all of them, anyway. How am I going to trace them?' She was impatient now for the woman to leave. As soon as she'd go, Emma wanted to start looking her up. What could be her past history? Did she always live alone and worked as a nurse? What if the answer was there? 'I really want it to be there,' Emma thought. 'Why? Who told me, by the way, that she lives alone? If she works on Saturday and Sunday mornings, it doesn't necessarily mean it. The first thing I should find out is who she works for,' Emma concluded. In her mind, she was sliding the pictures of that morning, when she first met the woman who called herself Val. A plastic ribbon around the station, indicating road works. The woman in the iron lattice chair next to her. The woman running fast away from her. The taxi, with her in it, going around the corner. The black scarf on the back of the chair. Her own hand stretched to grab the scarf. 'She's lying about the client who cut himself,' made Emma an obvious conclusion and sighed. 'What else do I know?' She switched off the light and locked the door, after having let Val out of it. Her day was finished now. She may know more tomorrow.

When Emma woke up the next morning, her first thought was about Val. She remembered her password and username, but somehow felt uneasy, thinking about reading her e-mails. She decided to call her friend Maud and ask what she thinks. 'If she thinks it's okay, we can do it together,' she thought. When Maud arrived at Emma's place, she looked very interested. 'You are investigating a murder case, are you,' she said. 'Murder? Whose murder?' 'I thought this is what we have to find out,' Maud answered. 'What else can it be, reasonably speaking? If it wasn't a murder, she wouldn't come to you to get her scarf back. She wouldn't leave it to you, or near you, in the first place.' 'I'm not sure I actually want to look into her e-mails,' Emma said. 'Somehow it makes me uneasy. It is intrusive, after all. Dishonest, too.' 'Rubbish,' Maud said. 'There is no other way to find out more, for us. Besides, just about everybody does it. It's actually normal.' 'If it's normal,' Emma objected, 'why then nobody would say that it's now normal? If nobody says so, what kind of norm is it?' 'It's a new kind of norm,' Maud said. 'I'd call it a clandestine norm.' 'Most really wicked people always have said that the end goal justifies the means, whatever they can be. Isn't it what you are suggesting?' 'Do you want to do it or do you not?' Maud said, 'it's getting tiresome.' 'I do,' Emma said. 'I just feel obliged to tell you about my scruples.' When a couple of minutes later Maud and Emma were looking at the list of senders in Val's inbox, they were disappointed. There was nothing, that would suggest an immediate answer to the murder question. 'I guess we'll have to open them all,' Maud said. 'Thank God most of them have the subject field filled. It'll let us sift through the obvious spam.' 'This one seems to be her close friend,' Maud said, pointing at a man's name. 'The subject he entered read 'tomorrow's date'. The e-mail was from somebody called Owen, whom Val appeared to see regularly. They usually exchanged e-mails, before meeting somewhere in town. 'Strange,' Maud said. 'Most people would text, I think, or make mobile calls.' 'Well, she didn't,' Emma said. 'I wonder why. But look, according to her inbox, they stopped seeing each other about a month ago. At least, they stopped sending e-mails.' 'What if it was him she killed?' Maud suggested. 'Kill him? Why?' 'How would I know? He seems like the most significant person in her inbox, doesn't it? But we need to know, why she's stopped seeing him. Let's look into the 'sent' folder.' There was nothing there, however, apart from the last of Val's rather uniform e-mails, confirming a date. It seemed like there was no explanation given by either side for a sudden break-up. At least, it wasn't among Val's e-mails. 'What if they quarrelled?' Maud said. 'They quarrelled and . . . and one of them got very aggressive.' 'Which one? We don't even know, what they are like. Let's have a look at what else is here.' 'Not much,' Emma, who had been opening e-mails all along, said. 'She was a nurse and worked for an agency. They sent her e-mails now and then. Mostly, when they had a new shift to offer her. Sometimes they were late with her pay for some reason and she'd e-mail the relevant person to enquire.' 'What, if she killed somebody she worked with?' Maud asked. 'What do you mean 'worked with?' Emma said. 'Somebody she looked after? Or her payroll officer?' 'I think, rather the latter than the former,' said Maud. 'If she killed somebody she looked after, she wouldn't be so anxious. Everybody makes mistakes. Besides, she is usually alone at her work site, that is, at the place of whoever she looks after, so there can't be any witnesses. Unless, of course, somebody is looking at her all the time,' Emma finished. 'You are obsessed,' Maud noticed. 'And anyway, I'm not sure it's the kind of evidence that can be used against her. No, I believe, if she killed somebody at work, it would be a person she worked under, or depended upon.' 'How can you kill your payroll officer?' Emma asked. 'And why? Your pay would be almost certainly delayed then.' 'I don't know, as to why,' Maud said. 'What, if she was romantically involved?' 'Romantically involved with a payroll officer? You really have a sick imagination. Besides, her payments wouldn't be delayed then, and they regularly were.' 'There is no question of how to kill. She could use a gun.' 'Did she have one?' 'We don't know. I think she could just come to the office, and pick up something heavy, like a vase, and kill him, you know.' 'I don't know,' Emma said. 'Wouldn't she be in jail then?' 'Not necessarily,' Maud said. 'It could be blamed on the person who bought those heavy vases, in the first place. It's against the occupational health and safety, you know.' 'You seem to be working too much,' Emma noticed. 'I think, if she killed somebody, it should have been for more personal reasons, than not being paid on time.' 'The answer lies in her break-up with this guy, what's his name again, Owen? I wonder, if we can ever find out, what was the reason.'

'I don't think there always has to be a reason,' Maud said. 'You know, yesterday I was lying on a sofa and watching TV, and suddenly noticed there was something new on top of my bookshelf. From underneath it looked like a little triangle pyramid, green and shiny. I figured it was a nicely glazed piece of ceramics and wondered, what it was. Although I wondered, I didn't take it off the shelf and have a better look. Perhaps, I just liked it, where it was. Then, when my sister came home, I asked her what it was.' 'So what was it?' Emma asked, looking intrigued. 'It turned out it was a nose, made of blue plastic, it wasn't ceramics, after all. It comes with a stick-on round plate and is meant to be stuck on the wall in whatever place you like it, like your bathroom.' 'Ah, I see.' 'What I mean, there doesn't have to be a reason, why they stopped seeing each other.' 'Possibly,' Emma said. 'Although I can't say, I've seen it happen often. But she would hardly kill him then, if it was like that, would she?' 'Then it wasn't him she killed,' Maud said. 'Does it follow from the story of you contemplating a strange object on top of your bookshelf that she didn't kill him? Anyway, let's have a look, who else she communicated with.' 'Let's.' Maud opened a few more e-mails. 'There isn't much. She had some relatives, I can't even make out where, they never say, and they e-mailed her now and then. Mostly about birthdays and stuff. She also shopped online, and when she ordered something, they'd e-mail her to confirm an order or a delivery date,' she said. 'What did she order?' 'Not much here,' Maud repeated. 'Mostly clothes. Sometimes health products like treadmills, but only very rarely.' 'Look,' Emma said, opening the 'sent' folder again. 'She sent an e-mail to somebody she ordered this treadmill from. Let's see what she wrote.' She opened an e-mail. 'Next time I see it, you will regret it, I promise. Don't make me do it,' it read. Emma looked excited. 'This is really something, isn't it?' she said. 'Sounds like a real threat. But what, I wonder, is 'it'? I mean, what did she mean by 'see it'?' 'Yes, it's a serious question,' Maud said. 'I wonder, is that treadmill working fine? I mean, if she bought something faulty, it would be easier to explain, why she was angry with it.' 'We can find out, if we go to her place and have a look,' Emma said. 'It would be wonderful,' Maud said, 'but who'd let us in?' 'We can have a look through the window. Or pretend to be somebody she'd always let in. Like a postman, you know.

Or cleaners. Or members of Jehovah witnesses. Even mormons.' 'Mormons are always male, but Jehovah witnesses can be women,' Maud observed. 'But I think, the most important problem is that she may open the door alright, but it doesn't mean she'd let us in, so we won't have a chance of seeing anything of interest. Jehovah witnesses is not a bad idea, you know. Of course, sometimes they are not even let in, but, at other times, they may score a conversation. I wonder, if she is this kind of person. But we better come, when she is not there, because, remember, she knows your face.'

'Okay,' Emma said. 'We'll pretend to be Jehovah witnesses. There is always a chance, that whoever is there, when she is not home, just won't open the door for them, that is, for us, at all. Of course, we must come, when she is out. We can actually do it on a Sunday morning, when we know, that she is at work. It's also the most likely day for Jehovah witnesses to come.' 'But who do you expect to open the door for us?' Maud said. 'I think, there's somebody else there,' Emma said. 'I passed by her house a couple of times in the last week, and I've seen male clothes on the line.' 'Have you actually seen him?' Maud asked. 'No,' Emma said. 'But he seems to be an ivalid. He has a special car. It's parked in the driveway.' 'We can probably find out who it is just by looking in the mail-box when letters are delivered,' Maud observed. 'It's too noticeable,' Emma said. 'If we go there as some kind of doorknockers we'll meet him anyway.'

When next Sunday morning Maud and Emma knocked on Val's door, nobody answered. 'She must be at work,' Maud said. 'I wonder where he is, however. You really have to be a bit of a masochist to be awake at this time.' 'He might have gone out for an early walk,' Emma said. 'There's nothing impossible about it.' 'Let's go around and knock on the back door,' Maud said. 'There's no harm in that, is there. They may even hear us better.' Three little steps were leading up to the back door, but when they knocked, again, nobody answered. An old wheelchair stood aligned with the porch, and Maud whispered to Emma. 'You are right, there's somebody else here.' She made two steps towards the window and looked in. 'I can't make out if there is somebody in this bed,' she said to Emma. 'Have a look.' 'I don't quite see it either, let's go,' Emma said. 'Wait,' Maud said. She tried the back door, and, miraculously, it was open. Emma wanted to come in. 'Wait. Let's find out when she comes back first,' Maud said. It wasn't difficult: the friends ordered coffee in a little café opposite Val's house and sipped it, until she came back at one o'clock in the afternoon. 'What, I wonder, we'd been doing if there was no café?' Maud said. 'We could meet her at the station,' Emma said. 'Although, of course, it's a bit more complicated because she could recognize me. I hope she'll be working tomorrow morning, too. Then we can come in through the back door, if she leaves it open again.' 'What if she doesn't?' 'We'll see.'

Everything turned out to be as Emma predicted. Val worked the next day too, and the back door was open again. It was around nine in the morning when Maud and Emma came into Val's house through the door. 'Let's see what's there in the bed,' Emma said. They came into the room they could see through the backyard window, but there was nobody in the bed. In fact, there were no sheets on it either. 'What did you expect,' Maud said 'the dead body?' 'I guess so,' Emma said. 'But look, there was one just a short time ago. These are the documents from a funeral company,' she pointed at a piece of paper on the table next to the bed. 'The dead man's name was Rex Clingon and he died, according to this, three weeks ago. It's two days before I met her at the station. It looks like the scarf definitely has something to do with it.' 'Why,' Maud said 'does she leave the back door open? Isn't it strange? Just anybody can come in and look through her things.' 'What if she does it on purpose? If anybody can come in, then anybody could be the person who killed him, if ever there is a doubt about it. It looks to me like she didn't want too many people to know he is dead. His clothes are on the line and the blanket on this bed is arranged as if somebody is sleeping under it. Why did she do it if she used a company to organize his funeral? It's a very public way.' 'I think,' Maud said 'she might be the person who changes her point of view quite often, especially, you know, in important situations or under stress. She disposed of that scarf at the station and then wanted to get it back. What do you think she used it for?' 'I guess, to wipe the blood. She could have stabbed him or hit with something heavy,' Emma looked around and sighed 'It's been a few weeks and whatever traces there might have been, I guess, are cleaned off and deleted now. His body, of course, contains a clue, but who can have an access to it? Certainly not us.' She looked around again and picked up something that looked like a small box from a chair. 'Look,' she said to Maud 'this certainly is a piece of luck.' 'What is it?' 'It looks like an electronic device of some kind to me,' Emma said 'and I think I know which kind, but let's check.' She pressed the 'on' button on the black box's control panel and a menu popped up on the screen. It read 'food; drinks; clothes; hygiene; entertainment; computer; appointments; routine.' 'What is it?' Maud looked both scared and surprised. 'Let's see,' Emma said and pressed the word 'food'. Another list appeared on the screen: 'bread; soup; steak; coffee; sugar; cereal; potatoes'. 'I see,' Maud said. 'He was paralysed and couldn't speak. This black box has lists that covered all areas of his life. What if he wanted something outside the list?' 'I don't know,' Emma said. 'Maybe it could be reprogrammed. Of course, if the only way he could express his wishes was to press one of the buttons, it must have brought some limitations with it. I wonder if it's true, however. Some people who have such boxes, do speak. Or have some other ways of communicating. Look,' she continued 'there is a button called 'other' here. I wonder what's under it.' She pressed 'other' and it read: 'change my medication; change my physician; gym; go to the country; I don't like my life anymore'. 'Gosh,' Emma said. 'It looks like he had a repertoire of things he could wish for if nothing else helped. And among them a suicide, if, of course 'I don't like my life anymore' is a will for suicide. Is it, what do you think?' 'I don't know, I guess, it can be,' Maud said. 'Does this thing have a memory? By the way, what about the treadmill? Have you found it?' 'It's in the other room,' Emma said. 'It seems to be fully functioning. She was using it herself. I think she wrote this threatening message we found in her 'sent' folder to put us on the wrong track. Or, maybe, she wasn't satisfied with the treadmill at some point. Anyway, she hardly killed them. He died, this Rex person, and I think it wasn't, most likely, a natural death.' 'So what about the memory? Does this device, what d'you call it, have it?'.

'I don't know,' Emma said. 'They are called 'augmented communication' devices. There are many different kinds. I don't know if they have a memory. They may, I guess. Why?' 'If she killed him, it would be interesting to see what was the last thing he asked for.' 'Right,' Emma agreed. 'If only we could find the instruction for this thing. Where do you think she might keep it?' 'Give it to me,' Maud said. 'I think I can find it, if it has a memory.' She took the black box in her both hands and spent a few minutes pressing buttons. Finally she said 'Here, have a look. It's got a memory, but it looks like it stores only the last ten commands he used. It also gives times when certain buttons were pressed.' 'What were they?' 'Food and drink in the morning, then a walk and a TV time. I guess all these were his usual things.' Emma was standing next to Maud now looking at the screen. 'Look, he pressed this 'no more like my life' button, too,' she said. 'Do you think she killed him because of this, to fulfil his wish?' 'Could be,' Maud said. 'I wonder if it's counted as euthanasia, however. Also, it can be that he didn't press it himself. She knew, most probably, that this thing has a memory, and if she was going to kill him, she could press it herself. But look,' Maud said 'he pressed another button at exactly the same time, the 'change my medicine' one. I guess, it means it was him, after all, pressing buttons. Perhaps he had motor problems, most these people do, and he might have missed the one he meant to press. If it was only one, that is. Sometimes people make their messages unclear on purpose. I guess, people who use these devices are no exception.' 'Gosh,' Emma breathed out 'this is all crazy. Do you think she killed him because he pressed the button? Crazy to have a button which means a death wish, don't you think?' 'Why? You can have any button you want,' Maud said. 'If people are supposed to wish for their own death, under some circumstances, there will be a button for it, obviously. But she didn't kill him because of the button. She probably got something from it, like an inheritance. I mean, if they shared this place, obviously she is not going to lose it, when he's dead. Who was he to her, by the way, have you found it?' 'No,' Emma said. 'I don't know. Does it matter? Let's go. I don't want to know anymore'. 'What happened,' Maud said 'is that she might have got angry with him for something. And thought what she was doing is OK, because he, or somebody, no matter who, pressed the button. She might have imagined it's perfectly legal, and then, perhaps, realized it's not.' 'What did she use to kill him?' 'I don't know,' Maud answered. 'It's too late to say now. I think what really matters is who pressed the button. But we can't ever tell, can we?'

The fence medium

'You know,' Emma told Maud when she called her up one Sunday evening, 'I've decided to quit my library job from tomorrow.'

'Really?' Maud sounded surprised, but not enough for Emma. She'd like her to be outraged. 'Why? What are you going to do now?'

'It's hard to say why,' Emma said. 'I guess I'm just tired. Or maybe the truth is I don't get along with people. Anyway, I've decided I'm going to become a busker now.'

'Become who?'

'A busker.'

'A street singer? What are you going to sing?'

'I'll be singing my own songs,' Emma said. 'Haven't I told you about them?'

'Not really,' Maud said. 'I've seen your novel, the one in the bag you've found, where was it? At the station? Anyway, that miss Prim's bag, but no songs.'

'It wasn't a miss Prim's bag at all,' Emma said. 'You misinterpret everything. Anyway, I've been writing lots of songs lately and I'm going to sing them. Why not? It seems a reasonable enough way to reach wide audiences. Come to hear me, I'll reach you too.'

'Where?'

'Where? I haven't chosen a place yet. I'll tell you when I have.'

'Does busking come from 'basques?' Maud asked. 'I mean, you know, you have an accent. Are you sure they'll understand you?'

'You are just trying to discourage me,' Emma said. 'Busking has nothing to do with 'basques', if you want to know. I think it comes from 'bass' rather than anything else.'

'From 'bass'? Doesn't it mean that buskers are supposed to be men, normally?'

'Not at all,' Emma said. 'In fact, it's not true. 'Busking', really, comes from 'bush'. It used to mean wandering around and picking up sticks for firewood in the bush. I think, they could be singing to avoid getting lost. And to entertain themselves.'

'I see,' Maud said. 'Do you expect to make any money, then?'

'I don't know. Why think about money now? I'll see when I pick up a place'.

Two weeks after this conversation Emma was well into her new idea. When Maud came to hear her at the station, where she was busking in the underway, she thought that things were going not that badly for her, after all. The station, one of the central ones, was called Holden Park.

'Why have you chosen this one of all?' Maud asked.

'It reminds me of the Catcher in the Rye,' Emma said. 'You know I like him. And also, because I like wry jokes. I even wondered, if I could do better, if I tell some.'

'Have you?'

'Not yet. I'm not yet sufficiently familiar with the singing situation. You know,' Emma continued, 'rye is a dietary requirement for me. That is, I'm not allowed to eat wheat, but they've found I can't, only a year and a half ago. Imagine what a genius I could have been, if they'd tell me about it before.'

'Hmm. I find you sufficiently unconventional as you are,' Maud said. 'There is no need to feed you rye to improve it.'

'By the way, I used to drive a Holden,' Emma said. 'You see, what rye means to me, do you?'

'I've read about all these catchers and stuff so long ago, I can't remember anything,' Maud said. 'You seem to be happy here,' she added, to change the subject. Before she went, she heard Emma to sing a song. It went like this:

What are you doing around the clock?
What else can it be? It must be paid work.

Pull the string of clockwork orange.
Add some water. Mix a porridge.

Don't forget to lock the door,
When you step into the mo.

Morning fog in Collins street.
A latte at dawn is sticky and sweet.

Its colour and smell
Remind me of something.
Of what? I don't know.
Perhaps, permacolour.
Or maybe of snow.
It can be compared, of course, to the fog
That covers the buildings away from a wog.

But speaking of latte.
What makes better sense?
To get out there and get all your cents
Depending on luck and somebody's good will
Depending, again, on . . . oh, what a treadmill!

Or else to depend on somebody else
And never get there to get any cents.
What's better? What's worse?

For better and worse,
For richer and poorer
You choose what to endure.

Choose a manager wisely.
Or be one and avoid all remorse.

Two days later Maud knocked on Emma's door in the morning. 'Look what I've found. I've found your song in this book,' she said under her breath. Emma was so sleepy, she couldn't feel sufficiently surprised.

'Where?' was the only thing she managed to mumble.

'I've found it in a bookstore, just yesterday. The name of the person who wrote it is, according to the cover, Shane Scrypher. It says in the introduction that he lived about one hundred fifty years ago, in England, and died in London in 1882.'

'But this is nonsense,' Emma protested. 'How can this be? What song have you found there?'

'The one I heard you performing yesterday. Or rather its words.'

'How can it be?' Emma asked again. 'Half these things and words for them just didn't exist then. Does it say where he lived?'

'As I said, he died in London. Perhaps, he lived there too. What words do you mean?' 'Words like 'manager'. How can they be in it, if it was written then? Or even 'latte?''

'Perhaps they meant something different then. Something like 'an ager of men', men ager, manager.'

Emma looked pensive for a minute or two. 'Perhaps I should say that we should try and find out as much as possible about this guy. Not that I know how to do it, however. We can't possibly start looking for things like birth certificates and other documents of the time, so what's left then? Especially if he never really existed which, I suspect, may be the case,' she said.

A week later it was Maud who was woken up by Emma.

'Listen,' Emma sounded unusually sinister. 'You know what happened just yesterday night? Somebody broke the fence in my front yard.'

'Uhm? How?' Maud could hardly speak at all.

'This is what I'd like to know too. When I went out onto the porch they've disappeared already.'

'Who they?'

'I said I don't know. Whoever it was who assaulted me.'

'Assaulted? It could have been an accident. Just a reckless drunk driver, you know. But it seems more likely to me, that it's your busking which is the reason.'

'Why?' Emma sounded genuinely surprised. 'I'm not singing anything that would sound extreme or provocative, am I? And you know yourself that some of it can be found in that volume by an obscure English writer who allegedly lived more than one hundred years ago. Do you think he was a revolutionary of some kind?'

'It's not what should be bothering you,' Maud said firmly. 'Look out for somebody you know who might have broken your fence. Something tells me, it wasn't just a drunk accident.'

'Okay,' Emma agreed. 'As soon as I find him, I let you know.'

And so she did. One day Emma called Maud. 'I think I've found him. Just yesterday I've seen a man in a supermarket with strangely spaced scars on his face. To tell the truth, the space between them was exactly the same as that between iron rods in my fence. I think it's him,' she said.

'What? What rods?'

'My fence, the one in the front yard, is made of iron rods,' Emma sounded impatient. 'And he had quite a few vertical scars across his face. I think there were four or even five. The space between them was, as far as I could estimate it, I mean, I couldn't measure it with a ruler, could I, the same, as it is between the rods in the fence that was broken.'

'What if the way he's acquired these scars, has nothing to do with your fence?'

'Do you think I could ask him? I'm not sure, if I can actually get to know him better, but, I think, I'll try. I really want to know what happened there.'

A few days later Emma ran into the man with a scarred face in the supermarket again. She managed to be close to his trolley in the queue waiting to pay. She dropped her wallet, and when he picked it up, predictably, she started a conversation. They went out together and Emma thought that, perhaps, she'd be able to find out as much as she wanted about him now. His name was Nick and he lived nearby, was thirty two years of age and worked for an insurance company.

'Would it be rude, if I ask about scars now,' Emma was thinking. 'Anyway, they can hardly do something with my fence. He couldn't be, seriously speaking, pushing face first against it, could he? But . . . These scars look so much as my fence . . .' Emma decided that she didn't know Nick well enough to ask about his face yet. Instead, he asked her out and she accepted.

Emma and Nick finished their food and were halfway through the dessert, when Emma decided it was time to ask personal questions. She made up a couple and finally got to the one that bothered her most.

'What's the most unusual thing about you?' she asked, staring intently at the equally spaced stripes on Nick's face.

'I'm not sure how to tell you,' Nick said. 'The thing is I'm a medium.'

'What does it mean?' Emma felt, that, perhaps, she expected something like this.

'I can tell things.' Nick said. 'Things other people don't know.'

'Really? What kind of things?'

'A lot of different things, but under one condition: they matter to me. Then I can make a necessary connection.'

'Can you tell me who broke my fence?' Emma asked.

'I can,' Nick said, 'but you know, I'd rather not. I'm working for an insurance firm, as you may remember, and there can be a conflict of interest.'

'Do you think I'll be able to claim it?' Emma asked the question that worried her most.

'You have to inquire about it in a regular way. Is it why you've agreed to go out with me?' he added.

'No, no,' Emma was slightly embarrassed. 'But do the scars in your face have anything to do with my fence? Because you see, when I first saw you, I thought that they look exactly like the rods in my fence do.'

Nick hesitated for a second. 'They are like, you know, kind of stigmata. I've been thinking so much about you and your fence, that they appeared. I've told you, I'm a medium,' he said.

'Why have you thought about me?'

'Perhaps I anticipated that you are going to ask me this question. You know, both on personal and professional levels.'

'I see,' Emma sighed. 'You know,' she said after a pause, 'there's something I'd like to ask you, since you are a medium. Not about the fence,' she said, firmly. 'Er . . . I've recently found my poem in a volume published by somebody else.'

'A poem? In somebody else's volume? What kind of poem is it? I'd never tell you write poems,' he added, as an afterthought.

'Why not?'

'I don't know. Perhaps the way you look doesn't quite agree with my idea of a poet. Although I must admit, I haven't known many.'

'Don't they make insurance claims? What do they usually claim for?' Emma sounded interested.

'I don't know. The usual stuff. Cars. Houses. I haven't met a single one who'd lodge a fence claim. Although, of course, there could be some people who won't admit they write poetry, when they claim. I'd say, it's wise.'

'What should they look like, according to you?'

'I don't know,' Nick looked like he felt uneasy. 'It's not something I can formulate clearly, but, definitely, not like you.'

'Can you tell me who wrote this book?' Emma got the volume Maud brought her, out of her bag and showed it to Nick.

'What do you mean who?'

'I mean, his name. Was it really this?' she pointed at the big bold words 'Shane Scrypher' printed on the cover.

'Does it matter?' Nick looked sceptical. 'There were no passports then, nor even driver's licenses.'

'I mean, was it the name other people used to call him?'

'Are you sure he was a real person?' Nick asked, too.

'I thought you might be able to tell me,' Emma said.

'Maybe I could, but I need to make a connection with this stuff first. It should matter to me. If, for example, we were both involved in this, and I was you co-author, or an editor, then, maybe, I'd be able to tell.'

'Wouldn't there be a conflict of interest for you, again?' Emma asked. 'Don't you think it would affect your judgment?'

'But in a good way.'

'Okay, let's try,' Emma said. 'You know, there is an old game, when one person says the first line of a poem, then another adds a second, then they cover up the first one, and the next person adds a line rhyming with the only line he sees—the last one. It's called bouts rimés or something similar. We can play something like this with my lines, too. Let's start with this one. 'What are you doing round the clock?' she read, almost singing the last 'o' in 'clock'.

Nick looked like he was thinking hard for a second and then said 'Today I'll be trying a new dainty frock.'

'Not bad, not bad at all,' Emma looked happy. 'It worked, you know. You can do it. But why 'dainty frock'? Do you have a gay somewhere deep inside you?'

'I rather think not,' Nick blushed a bit, as he was saying it. 'I was just thinking of myself as you, that's all. It is yourself you are asking all these questions about the clock, right?'

'I don't know,' Emma said. 'I don't think so. But your line is good, anyway.'

'Most gay feelings come from reading books,' Nick looked like he wanted to explain more. 'Since it's written by men, the reader looks at everything and everybody through their eyes, and . . . you see . . . In your case it's quite the opposite,' he concluded. He thought about something for a moment and added, 'But if you don't like 'frock', we can try something else. How about 'undress and try another cloak?' It's too, what do they call it, raw, isn't it?' he added.

'I see,' Emma said. Suddenly she felt very sad. 'Can you tell me now what the person who wrote this volume was like? This poem is in it, you see,' she opened the book on page 134 and showed it to Nick.

'Well, not quite,' he mumbled. 'I'm just starting to make a connection. What else do you have in your wretched, pardon me, poem?'

'Why wretched? It's one of my favourites in my oeuvre. That is, in what I considered, so far, to be my oeuvre. I've even made a song out of it and sing it when I'm busking. The next line goes like this: 'Pull the string of clockwork orange.' What would you add to this?'

'The clock again,' Nick said. 'You seem to be a really anxious person to me. You can't put two words together, without mentioning the clock. I don't know any words rhyming with orange, do you?'

'Not many,' Emma agreed.

'How about Solange,' Nick was, apparently, thinking aloud. 'It's a girl's name, isn't it? Or, maybe, 'courage'? Something like 'Don't be afraid and feel the courage', but it doesn't really rhyme with the first one.'

'Orange—courage. No,' Emma nodded. 'It doesn't.'

'Or, maybe, pull the spring of clockwork orange, find the place to get your forage.'

'Can you tell me now who wrote the volume?' Emma interrupted.

'You see, there are a few possibilities,' Nick said. 'The first one, of course, is that somebody has liked your favourite poem so much that they decided to publish it under a different name. In other words, stole it.'

'Why?'

'What do you mean why? There are two main reasons. It could be either for profit, or out of vanity, or maybe both. Strictly speaking, there can be another reason. If they anticipated you'd be so distressed about it, it could be the reason too. Just out of spite.'

'I don't have any enemies,' Emma said, solemnly. 'And this author, according to the foreword, is supposed to have been dead for more than a hundred years. So it can hardly be his vanity or his profit.'

'It could be somebody else's. Whoever it is behind this enterprise will get a profit. And, if it was your name on the cover, it would be a different story.'

'Why?'

'Because it's less marketable, than somebody's who's already dead or, maybe, has never existed. You can assign plenty of good traits to a dead person and even more to an imaginary one. As for you, what kind of author figure makes a middle-aged librarian with an accent?'

'What does it matter, if I'm middle-aged?' Emma protested. 'A secretary has to be young and presentable, although I don't quite see why, and a model, too. Perhaps there are some other jobs, where it's important. But why should it matter in a writer?'

'I don't know,' Nick said, 'but it does. Perhaps it makes them more promising, if nothing else.'

'I see,' Emma said. 'What about the other possibilities? What are they?'

'Well,' Nick looked rather uncertain of what he was going to say. 'I don't know how to tell you. I think it's actually possible that two people should think of the same thing. It does happen. And if they think of the same thing, they can write the same thing, too.'

'In exactly the same words?'

'Well, it depends,' Nick was mumbling and seemed very reluctant to go on. 'It depends,' he said again. 'Depends on what words they are. How unlikely, do you think, is that two people would write a phrase like 'what are you doing around the clock?' independently?'

'I don't know,' Emma said, feeling that she must say something.

'It's not very unlikely,' Nick answered his question himself. 'It's a question lots of people ask. That's the reason why they use this phrase, 'round the clock'.

'I see,' Emma said. 'And then?'

'And then the person who'd made up this line would think of another. As you've seen yourself, there are a few possibilities here. Most people wouldn't pick up the same second line, as you did. But somebody may.'

'Who?'

'I don't know,' Nick said. 'Somebody who was a lot like you. Exactly like you. Around the clock.'

'But lived a hundred and fifty years ago and died, before my grandmother was born. D'you think it's possible?'

'Do you feel you are so much defined by when and where you live?' Nick asked, in his turn. 'It's no good. In what way?'

'Because I've to work,' Emma said. 'Obviously, it makes me different from people back then who didn't. And also, because I moved countries in the middle of my life.'

'You know,' Nick said, 'it happens that two people who live completely different lives look exactly the same. Do you think it means something?'

'Possibly,' Emma said. 'I've never met any pairs of such people. I mean, apart from twins and close relatives. A friend of mine showed me her picture once and that of her grandmother. When she was three, I mean, when both of them were, they looked exactly the same. But later—no. Not anymore. It can be that people coincide, just for a short while, and later they diverge. I mean, in their looks. Do you think they say the same thing at this point of coincidence?'

'It could be. It would seem natural. What, if you coincided with this guy here?'

'He was a man, according to the foreword to this book,' Emma said, appalled. 'And apart from that, what do I have in common with him? Can you actually establish a connection? Bring him here?'

'I'll try,' Nick promised. 'But not today. It's enough for today.'

Emma and Nick met two days later at Emma's place. 'I'm ready to bring this guy here for you. You can talk to him. I mean, it will be through me, of course, physically, but in fact it'll be him you are going to talk to,' Nick told her.

Emma felt she is so happy, it was even scaring her.

'Fine,' she said, 'Let's start right now'. When Emma and Nick sat down at her dining table opposite each other, she went straight to the point.

'Who are you?' she asked.

'My name is Lisa,' Nick said in a voice very different from his normal one. 'I'm twenty one.'

'Lisa?' Emma wasn't sure she heard it right. 'Aren't you Shane? The guy from the cover of my volume?' She showed the book to Nick again, although she wasn't sure, that in his Lisa's capacity he can see it. In his own, on the other hand, he already had. But just in case.

'I'm Lisa,' Nick repeated. 'Shane Scripter is my pen name. It was easier to write under an assumed name in those days.'

'So you are a kind of George Sand,' Emma said. Nick as Lisa's impersonation ignored this remark.

'What's your last name, Lisa?' Emma asked.

'I'm Lisa Vendetta,' Nick said.

'Vendetta? What are you, Italian? How come?' Emma was getting more and more surprised.

'Not Vendetta,' Lisa corrected. 'It's vedetta. You know, it means something like a movie star, although it used to mean a tower, from which soldiers could observe their enemies approaching the city. Both come from 'see', you know. Although, of course,' Lisa continued, 'vendetta' may be related to these observation towers, too.'

'You certainly know a lot about it, Lisa,' Emma said. 'How come you've written your poem in English?'

'I've come to England on Titanic,' Lisa said.

'Titanic? Was it then?' Again, Nick, or rather Lisa in his body, didn't answer this question. Suddenly Emma found herself searching for another question.

'How did you die?' she asked.

'My sister died,' Lisa said, 'when I started singing my songs in the street. They've killed her, you know. And then I realized that, perhaps, I'm the only person around, who doesn't see, what's right and wrong. Vendetta can't be right, if you've got relatives. They may have to pay dearly for it, you know. So I've changed my name for Vedetta.'

'I see,' Emma said.

'But Lisa Vedetta didn't work very well, either. And in the end I picked up, or rather, they did for me, that other name.'

'I see,' Emma said. 'Who were they?' It was perhaps, the most interesting question, but something must have changed already. 'It was nice to have met you, Emma. I must go now,' Nick said in a voice, bordering on his normal one. Then he breathed in deeply and said to Emma, 'So? How did you find her?'

How Emma did her tax return

When the end of the financial year came again, Emma jumped on her bike and went to see a tax agent. His door, she noticed previously, was hospitably open on the corner of two major roads nearby. She got off her bike and leaned it against the wall, but it fell down. She thought vaguely: 'it may be better this way, if he can't see it out of the window' and also 'what a hot summer there was', and came in. There was a nice friendly looking man inside. When he asked how he can help her, she presented her question.

'I'm not going to lodge a tax return this year,' she said 'because I just wasn't working. I fell below the tax threshold. But somebody told me that I can claim the price of the computer I bought as an education tax refund. Is it true?'

'Sure,' the man told her. 'That's right. Come in before the end of the month and I'll do it for you for twenty dollars.'

Emma thanked him and went to the door. The man looked out, saw her bike lying in the footpath and said:

'Oh, you have a bike here. Healthy, isn't it?'

'What a sensible man,' Emma thought, riding back home.

For a couple of weeks that followed she was happy in the knowledge that if everything went so wrong with that computer she bought, at least, she can claim its price back. The computer was meant to be used for a program that helped people with ADD. Her son had ADD. Or at least, this was what Emma thought he had, because officially he had worse labels than that on him. The thing is – Emma thought – children with ADD can be very difficult in class and schools seek funds to support that in the way they can. But no funds are intended to go to those who are called 'ADD sufferers' or whatever it is they call them. They get them only if they call it something else, something more serious and sinister. Emma also believed, quite irrationally perhaps, because she couldn't tell why, that although those labels meant generous government payouts, they actually made people function worse. Perhaps not everybody was equally receptive to this, but many people were. Generally speaking, it was, perhaps, true that if a child was jumping in a classroom instead of sitting at a desk, this situation couldn't be just left as it is. But if a child and his parents were told that this was happening because the child has ADD rather than the reason is that he just can't understand what's going on around, it would be better for them all. The first thing, that is. It was hard, she thought, to distinguish one thing from another, especially for those children who were, in fact, foreign, and many of them were. However, there were many specialists who specialised in drawing this kind of distinction. It did happen that on the way to this distinction they had to employ a translator to speak to a supposedly abnormally inattentive child, and this translator could have an opinion and an attitude of his own, or just couldn't quite see what it was all about. Still, the important distinction should always be made. Needless to say, when Emma and her son had to go through this procedure of distinguishing one possible reason for jumping in a classroom from another, the verdict was a bad one.

But Emma continued to believe her own thing, as usual.

The computer program she bought was meant to take care of all of this, but it didn't work. Or, rather, it worked for a little while, and then stopped. Who was responsible for this, she didn't know. There were too many possibilities. She went through the stages of acute anger at whoever might have been doing this, stubborn persistence when encountering each next problem she would visit the person she got it from and get another technical consultation, and then, in the end, indifference. Nothing helped. She wasted time and money asking constantly for technical support, but it didn't work anyway. After all, there might be other ways to address the same problem—she decided.

One thing she changed immediately, when the program stopped working, was to cancel her casual work. What did she need it for, if the program didn't work anyway? Wouldn't it be better to stay where she was and to look for other ways to deal with that attention problem?

She asked herself many times if it wouldn't be different if she had some kind of real work instead of her casual shifts helping people who had paralysis. Possibly, or maybe not. Perhaps, it depended on who was doing what with her wretched computer and this was something she didn't know. Or maybe, she decided, and it certainly made her feel better, it works the other way round. I don't have any real work because if I had it, I would spend any money I had on this kind of thing, and it's definitely not approved of. By whom? 'God only knows,' she thought 'but definitely by somebody who has enough power to stop it happening. Is using this kind of program not approved of in my case only,' she wondered 'or generally?' She suspected that it may be the case generally, especially for those wretched people who at a certain stage had the misfortune to put a bad label on themselves, usually looking for funds. Quite often schools pushed them, because it was them who needed funds. Those people fell within the grind and grid of the disability system, and this was it. After all, if everybody will be able to change themselves, what good verdicts made by specialists were? Perhaps it was the reason why places that provided this kind of equipment had their own specialists.

'Whatever causal links one could observe and describe in all this,' Emma thought 'it was the system, and what good could it do her to fight the system? But it was kind of stupid' she thought—to throw away a thousand dollars 'I must get it back.' It seemed easy to claim it, if that little friendly man from the corner taxation shop was going to help her. He said he would.

When a couple of weeks later Emma finally decided it was time to visit the little friendly tax man on the corner, she put the income statement for the year and the receipt for the computer in her bag, and put on her best coat, too. After she'd finish with the tax man, she was going to do some errands.

'Hello' she said in the apparently empty room when she got through the door. A second later the friendly man from the last time came into the room from behind the screen.

'How can I help you?' he asked.

'I'd like to ur . . . ' she said. 'Remember, I said I want to claim an education tax refund although I'm not claiming the tax return this year. I've brought my paperwork with me.'

'We are not doing this kind of thing,' the tax agent said. 'No. You can download the form from the internet yourself.'

'Yeah, I know,' Emma said. 'But it's too complicated. You said you can do it for me, remember?'

'We don't do it,' the tax agent said again. 'But I can give you the form to fill. For twenty dollars.'

'Yes, please,' Emma said. 'I would be most grateful.' The man brought the printed form from behind the screen and gave it to her.

'You can have it for free,' he said. 'Send it to this address,' he highlighted it with a texta.

'Oh thank you so much,' she said. She looked through the form. 'It does seem pretty straightforward,' she added. 'I think I can do it.'

'Wait,' said the tax agent. 'I can help you to fill it for twenty dollars, if you like.'

'Really?' Emma said. 'That would be good. Yes, please do.'

Why did she say it? Did she really still want help? Perhaps she believed she'd get her money sooner if he helps her. And it would be kind of embarrassing to refuse to accept his help, didn't she ask for it twice herself? She vaguely thought that the man started by saying he doesn't want to help her and didn't think it was embarrassing even though he previously said he would. 'He must know what's the right way to behave under the circumstances,' flied or rather slowly floated through her head.

'Yes, please,' she said.

'What's that?' the tax agent said, pointing at the folder she put before him.

'This is my income statement,' Emma said. 'And this is a receipt for a computer I bought for educational purposes. You see' she continued 'I didn't do much casual work this year. Just a thousand dollars. And here you see' she pointed at the receipt 'I spent this thousand on the computer, but the program I bought it for didn't work. So I want, at least, to get it back now.'

The tax agent frowned.

'What's your name?' he said. When Emma spelt her long foreign-sounding name, 'Are you happy with it?' he asked.

'What do you mean?' she asked, too. 'It's who I am. It's in my other passport. Besides, if I changed it, you'd be asking me now if I did, and how many times.'

'What's you hourly rate?' the tax man asked. This question wasn't on the form, she noticed. She also noticed suddenly his unusual accent. Was it cockney, perhaps? She didn't think she could ask it. 'Gosh, which one of us is Eliza here and who the hell is Pickering? I must be Eliza,' she decided.

'Hourly rate? Twenty dollars,' she said.

'I get one hundred an hour just for people looking at me,' He smiled at her, stretched his arm across the table between them and was now shaking her arm with his fingers.

'Is this classified as harassment?' Emma thought. She was really angry now. 'Perhaps not, he's really old and very respectable. Besides, where would I go with it? He's an independently operating something.' Emma freed her arm from his fingers and he said:

'Plenty of work in Melbourne, plenty. When I first came here . . . '

'Where did you come from?' she interrupted. 'England?'

'Yeah,' he said. 'I'm a Londoner.'

'I must have guessed right,' she thought. 'He is a cockney.'

'Are you from Czechoslovakia?' he asked?

'No,' Emma said. 'I'm Russian. Why?'

'I've had another lady from Czechoslovakia today,' the tax man said. 'She had the same problem.'

'Did she also lodge only an ed tax?' Emma asked.

The tax man didn't answer and suddenly pointed at her leather coat.

'Did you buy this in Russia?' he said. He smiled, but looked at her accusingly as if it was obvious to him that her story couldn't be true and the coat was the evidence. Emma felt offended.

'Do you think it's impossible to buy a leather coat in Russia?' she said. 'Why? As a matter of fact, I bought it in Italy, many years ago. Why?'

'OK,' he said. 'You can claim half the price of the computer on this box. Put five hundred in this box. Is there anything else you want to claim?'

'No,' she said. 'Just this thing. I can't just throw away a thousand dollars. It would be stupid and kind of irresponsible.'

'Anything else?' he repeated. 'Textbooks? Notebooks? Stationery?'

'No,' she said. 'It's just little things, and I don't have receipts for them anyway.'

'Textbooks?' he repeated.

'Gosh,' she thought. 'He seems to know for sure what I have. How? Or am I just paranoid?'

'No,' she said. 'No, thank you.'

'Sign here,' he said. 'But I can't sign and can't lodge it for you.'

'Why?' she asked. 'But you have completed it, haven't you? I thought you'd lodge it for me. Shouldn't you have told this to me earlier? I would be out of here and doing my own thing long time ago.'

'What do you want to do?' he said. 'Most people,' he added 'come here because they find it difficult to fill the form. May be you are different . . . '

'But I said I can do it,' Emma said. 'I thought, if you'll do it, you'll lodge it. The whole exercise has been misleading to me.'

'Ok,' he said, 'I can do it for you for eighty dollars. Online, of course.'

'Yes,' Emma said. 'Please, let's do it. How long will it take? No, I must be sensible,' she thought a second later. 'He is just playing with me, testing all kinds of possibilities.'

'Well, thanks,' she said. 'Here is your pay,' she put the note on the table.

'It completely doesn't make any sense to work here, in this city. You never get what you're doing it for, anyway,' Emma said, when she was leaving the tax man office.

A second later when she got through the door into the street, she realised that 'completely' should have been placed, of course, somewhere else. It could never be stuck between 'it' and the auxiliary 'doesn't'. Was it the reason why it all went so horribly wrong? From experience she knew that it was unlikely to be the root.

Is cake decorating a vice or a virtue?

'Have you ever seen a prostitute?' Maud asked Emma, as she had a habit to do, in a café.

'Probably, yes, from a distance. I suppose I drove by. You know, there are some areas where they just stand in the street. Why?'

'Do you think there can be prostitutes among students?' Maud asked again.

'Students? I don't know. Why?'

'I just heard about it, read in a newspaper, and started wondering. You know how anything that has something to do with sex is exciting to most people. I am no exception.'

'Do you think we could find a real prostitute somewhere and talk to her?' Emma said. 'It'd be curious. Where do they flock?'

'How easy it is to find one depends on what you count as prostitution. You know Engels, he was Carl Marx' best friend, he said that any marriage is prostitution.'

'Marriage? Why?'

'Because it is based on a marital contract and as a result women have a monetary benefit from their sex relations with their husbands.'

'What a nonsense!' Emma cried.

'He didn't think so. He advocated the communality of wives in communities and the elimination of marriage.'

'Did they get to it at all?' Emma asked, apparently thrilled.

'Who they?'

'I don't know. Communists. Communities.'

'No. As far as I know, not. The closest they ever got to it was a ban on religious marriages and church ceremonies. But this happened mostly because they didn't support the religion in general, not because of Engels' ideas on marriage. It was very easy to register a marriage in the first few years after the Revolution. You could do it in a moment, right on the spot. But the communality of wives . . . No. They didn't go that far.'

Maud and Emma kept silent for a while. They were thinking about different things. Maud was trying to imagine what the communality of wives would look like. Emma was thinking where to find an acting prostitute and get well acquainted with her. After a pause, Emma spoke.

'I suppose', she said, 'if we want to find a prostitute among a group of people, we should do the usual.'

'The usual what?' asked Maud.

'Look into their spending and bank accounts. If somebody has large sums of money, especially cash, unaccounted for, they are a suspect.'

'Fair enough', agreed Maud.

After scanning the spending regime of a good many people, Maud and Emma found a plausible suspect. It was an apparently normal woman in her forties who always spent more than what was deposited in her bank account.

'How do we handle it?' asked Maud, worried. 'How can we find out more?'

'Let's just approach her and ask where the money she spends comes from', said Emma.

And so they did. Ausla was an easy-going and talkative woman.

'You want to know where my resources come from?' she said. 'I'll tell you. It's the pleasant consequences of a lawsuit. I'd been working in a nursing home for a while and everything went well for me. Except for the fact that I was paid less that what a minimal wage is supposed to be. Just five bucks an hour. Then, after a while, I got fed up with it, and claimed the difference.'

'How?' asked Maud.

'Through one of those commissions which work to resolve things like this. They turned out to be quite helpful.'

'Listen, but five bucks an hour is like slavery', Emma said. 'How did you ever agree to it?'

'I can't remember now', said Ausla. 'Anyway, slavery is a form of labour which is altogether unpaid for.'

Ausla thought for a second and added.

'This is quite an optimistic and an easy to tell story, but one thing is sad about it.'

'What thing?' asked Maud and Emma, both together.

'When I got the difference, it was paid by cheque that I cashed, of course, immediately. But it looks like a person with lots of unaccounted for cash (is it lots, by the way? and is it unaccounted for?) is likely to be a suspect in a lot of bad things, including even prostitution. It doesn't make much difference whether you slave somewhere for virtually nothing and then claw and squeeze your dues out of your employer, or you trod the street', Ausla was nearly crying now.

'Calm down, you got your dues, haven't you?' said Emma.

'What are you going to do about it?' asked Maud.

'What do you think I am going to do?' Ausla was wiping tears. 'Ignore it, I guess. I'm not rich enough to do anything else.'

'She is nice, but not what I wanted ', said Emma. 'I want to see a real prostitute, don't you?'

'Yeah, why not', said Maud. 'Let's widen our mental horizons.'

Soon after they found another candidate. Her name was Tarta and she also spent more than she could account for.

'Let's do it differently this time', said Maud. 'If we approach her and ask direct questions, we'll know only as much as she wants us to know. Let's follow her and see what we can find out. We can always ask her later.'

They've been following Tarta for a week now, and, in Maud's and Emma's opinion, she did all the things a normal person would do. She cooked food and looked after her children (she had two), went for walks and came back with seedlings that she planted in her garden. She loved shopping and had two shopping days in a week. She didn't have a job that would pay for it, but, when you come to think of it, she didn't have any time for it either.

Then, after a while, Tarta finally did something less ordinary. Maud and Emma were observing her through a telescope (which they put in a window of a house right opposite the one where Tarta lived), when they saw that Tarta put a strange object made of worn out stained cotton and plastic into her bag. After this, she started getting dressed.

'She is getting ready to leave', Emma noticed. 'Where do you think she is going? What's that in her bag?'

'We'll have to find out, where', answered Maud. 'The thing in her bag is just a cake decorating syringe. Haven't you ever seen one? It's a cloth bag which has an opening at the bottom. The opening is made of something harder than cloth and looks like a nozzle. If you want to make cream or custard roses on your cake, all you need to do is to put whipped cream in the syringe bag and squeeze it out through the nozzle into the shape of a rose. Simple, but very efficient. You'd never make a cream rose to look like one without it.'

'Let's get up the stairs and see what's there', said Maud. 'Or we'll never know'.

'It can be dangerous', Emma observed. 'What if she comes out and sees us?'

'She won't suspect anything anyway. She's never seen us before, so even if she sees us in the staircase now, she won't know we are following her'.

Maud and Emma went one flight of stairs up, and found a door. It was made of some kind of plastic material which looked very much like glass.

'Put the dark glasses on and have a look at what's inside', Emma whispered to Maud.

Maud put her dark glasses on and peered through the door. What was behind it, surprised them enormously. It was a cake factory. Neat and tidy round sponge cakes were delivered by a moving strip every thirty seconds and decorated at the table by a team of women-cake decorators. Each woman held a cake syringe like the one Tarta put in her bag when she left home. Roses, frilly leaves and letters flowed out of the women's cake syringes, without a stop.

'Look, she does have a job, after all', Emma could hardly speak in her amazement. 'She works in a cake factory. I wonder how much they get here in an hour. It can't be five bucks, can it?'

'All this cream looks too dark through the dark glasses', noticed Maud. 'Do you think I can take them off and have a proper look?'

'Yeah, but do it quick and let's run.'

Maud took her glasses off and sneaked a glance at the cakes and cream, as they looked naturally.

'Quick, they'll notice', Emma reminded. Maud put the glasses back on and they rushed back home.

When Tarta finished her work, she checked once again if the cream syringe was in her bag, checked the keys in her purse, and left. At the station, she took a train to the city. Maud and Emma were following her, sitting in the next carriage.

'Where do you think she is going?' Emma asked again. An idea suddenly hit her brain and she said.

'Can you actually administer drugs through a cream syringe?'

'I don't think so', said Maud. 'But we'll see. Who knows what she may be up to'.

'What if she has an affair and is going to see her lover now?' Emma said.

'Yeah, it's possible, theoretically speaking,' Maud said. 'But you know . . . I kind of feel it's not the case . . . She doesn't . . .'

'Why?' Emma asked again. 'Why not? What makes you sure?'

'I don't know . . .' Maud mumbled. 'She is so pressed for time all the time . . . And mobiles . . . You know it's impossible to keep anything secret these days. I think it makes affairs highly unlikely, or vulnerable, at least.'

'How can you have an affair if you don't have a mobile?' Emma retorted.

'Nonsense', Maud said. 'There were no mobile phones just fifteen years ago or so. But people lived no less normal lives.'

'So you think there can't be any romance any more because of mobile phones?' Emma summed it up.

'Yeah. More or less so. Not just mobile phones. It's everything. Well, I mean, if I was a teenager, maybe I wouldn't care how many people can hear my amorous chatting on the mobile. Possible . . . Although I can't really imagine it. But as it is . . . And she is not a teenager, is she?'

Half an hour later, Tarta got off the train at the Flagstaff station. She took the escalator up, and then turned into one of the small streets. Maud and Emma followed at a distance. When Tarta went through a small dark door into one of the buildings, Maud and Emma waited for a few minutes behind the corner of the same building, and then came close. But however hard they tried, they couldn't see anything through the door.

Maud and Emma go to Merlin

Maud and Emma decided that their next investigation adventure should happen somewhere in a new place. In fact, they have wanted to go to Germany for a long time: they desperately wanted to seek and find somebody there. And it would make for a nice story, too. After all, Europe spells sophistication, doesn't it, although of course it can be all too much.

However, later Maud began hesitating and considering. How can they go to Germany—neither she nor Emma spoke any German. In fact, they couldn't read German, either. If you can't even read shop signs and banners, what on Earth can you understand in a place? But one can claim that it sharpens one's intuition. Maud considered, just momentarily, reviving a little knowledge of German she acquired as a second year student years ago. Perhaps it could help with the idea. But why bother? If you think about the way you would present your story to other people, it makes sense to try and imagine: would they like it, if the narrator speaks (a lot of) German? Would they actually be able to empathise with it? Or would they rather prefer a person who doesn't speak a word of German? Now, what if it wasn't German? Would it be any different? French? Italian? Greek? Russian? Would it be all the same for people in New York or Bejing? Maud sighed. She was a calm and balanced, one could say, a cold-blooded person. Whatever her blood was, however, it was such that she got too emotional when she thought about this 'language and place' question. It would take some research to find out, she decided. But it wasn't the easiest project to fund. So, in the meantime, she decided to go to Germany as she was. Forget about German, who needs unnecessary detail. And besides, she could always present her story as fantasy. Her Berlin would be Merlin—just a little bit like the city known to people who live there. It makes it even more interesting.

A couple of weeks later, Maud and Emma scraped some funds and bought themselves two tickets to Merlin. A week later their plane landed there and they got off it as happy as two people, or rather, two persons, can be (respectively).

It should be explained here what they came to Merlin for. The reason for their trip was a wish to investigate a well-known story. The person they wanted to find has recently become something like a legend. Her name was Hanna, and according to the legend, she was a Jew and a guard in an SS concentration camp during the World War II. The friends really wanted to meet her, or, if this proved impossible, to gather as much information as they could, from people who knew her or their relatives.

'How old can she be now, to begin with?' Emma asked.

'If she was, let's say, at least twenty in 1941, she would be now eighty eight,' Maud said. 'It is not impossible, of course, that she is alive, but it is at least as likely that she isn't. But if she was older, than twenty, then, she would be almost certainly dead now. So we'll have to go by testimonies of somebody who knew her. How, I wonder, could we find them?'

'It seems natural to contact some relevant organizations,' Emma suggested. 'Jewish. Maybe, a synagogue? How many people like Hanna who collaborated in this way, there were, anyway? I mean, if it's true, and it probably is, that she was such a rare animal, then any relevant organization would know about her.'

'Another thing to try,' Maud said, 'is court proceedings and archives. But we would need a permission to use it, so it's easier to imagine what we would find there. No fuss. I wonder, did they document what happened to every single person involved? Even a little person like Hanna?'

'I don't know,' Emma said. 'And I'm afraid not too many people know it at all. What we can always rely on, however, is word of mouth. If anybody like her ever lived, she would have had contacts. Younger relatives. But wait, if she didn't have children, who are they? And there were work colleagues, of course. But most of them would be dead by now. Their descendants would do, I suppose. Friends and neighbours. They can remember something, too. How can we find any of them, if she is, probably, dead?'

'Let's advertise,' Maud said. 'In a local newspaper. We'll start something like a focus group. You know, in market research they organize a focus group if they want to hear everything people could say about a product. What attracts you to this brand of shampoo? What are its best qualities? What is it you don't like about it? We can do just the same and see what people think and are willing to tell.'

'Of course, there is a risk that somebody will claim they knew our Hanna, when in fact they didn't and are making it up. But it's always like this with any interesting character who lived in the past. I don't think it should stop us.'

The notice Maud and Emma placed in the newspaper read: 'Desperately seeking friends, relatives and former colleagues of Hanna Ashmitz. Will appreciate any kind of information. If you have any information and are interested in taking part in our project, the aim of which is to establish the history of collaboration between the local Jewish community and SS during WWII, please call 1932-06-22-2000.'

The notice was written, of course, in the language spoken in Merlin—Merlinese German.

The first person who answered Maud and Emma's ad was an old man called Fritz. He came to the office they hired in the very heart of Merlin, leaning heavily on his wooden cane. Fritz sat down, and looked expectantly at Emma. Apparently, there was nothing he was eager to tell her.

'How did you first meet Hanna?' Emma asked.

'I first met her when I went to buy a newspaper in the morning' he answered.

'Where was it?'

'In the local convenience store.'

'What work was she doing then? How did you know it was her?'

'She was carrying too many things and dropped a purse. I picked it up and she thanked me. I introduced myself. In the evening of the same day we went to the pictures. This was out first date. We'd been dating for about a month after this.'

'What was she doing then, did you know?' asked Maud.

'I am not sure' Fritz sighed. 'I wasn't much interested. I think she was working in a coffee shop—in Stutgart Strasse. Or, wait, she was something like a lollipop lady in a school around there. Or was at a different time? I am not sure.' He looked lost.

'Did they have lollipop ladies at school then?' asked Emma. 'Was there a need? Was there as much traffic?'

'I am not sure,' Fritz repeated. 'I am sure she had a uniform, with SS embroidered on her collar. What it stood for, I am not sure. Perhaps—Stutgart Strasse—this is where the bakery was.'

'What about another SS? The Nazi one?' Maud asked. 'Did she work for them, too?'

'I don't know, girls,' Fritz said, happy and relaxed. 'Maybe. I'd known her only for a month and have no idea what she was doing before and after. I know the uniform she had was that of the Stutgart Strasse bakery.'

'We are really lucky to have found him, I mean, he is somebody who really knew her. If it was her, of course,' Maud said, when he left.

'If we knew a bit of German,' Emma said, 'maybe we could think of other word combinations that can be abbreviated as SS. Perhaps mix-ups like this one were quite common then? Or could they be? Are they now?'

'If we knew German, we could tell,' Maud said. 'But somehow it didn't happen. It's a shame, isn't it?'

Femme Fatale

Maud and Emma sat down in a café. 'You know there is something I want to tell you about. I got a really strange e-mail yesterday. It said they found a dress, nobody knows whose. In a room. The room is on the floor where I work,' Maud said.

'Oh,' Emma said. 'Really? What kind of dress? Why did they tell this to you?'

'I don't know,' Maud sighed. 'Perhaps, they think the dress could be mine, and this is why they sent a letter to me. But it's hard to imagine how one can lose a dress in a room. I mean, literally. Whatever happens, you can't leave without a dress, can you? On the other hand, may be, say, a student had been shopping in the morning and bought a dress, and then later in the day came to see her mentor. They have had a meeting and a bag with a dress was just forgotten on the floor where she dropped it. It could happen, couldn't it?'

'Yes,' Emma said. 'Why not. Imaginable. What kind of dress was it?'

'The e-mail says it's a mesh dress with white spots.' 'What d'you mean white spots?' Emma asked. 'Spots of what? Or do you mean polka dots?'

'Hard to say,' Maud answered. 'Of course, if it's printed, they should be called polka dots. If it's dirt, however, they are spots. But how can it be white?'

'And mesh, too,' Emma added. 'When was the last time you've seen a mesh dress? What is mesh used for, anyway?'

'Mesh is just a transparent cloth,' Maud said. 'There is cheese mesh. Or a tulle mesh, for curtains. In times bygone, they used mesh for making veils on hats. Of course, not many people would wear a mesh dress. It's transparent, you know. By the way, a friend of mine used to say that modesty and a transparent dress are two things that make a girl beautiful.'

'I'm not sure this kind of humour is appreciated here,' Emma said. 'This piece of wisdom should be rephrased, for the circumstances: Modesty and an appropriate dress make a girl beautiful.'

'Speaking of appropriate,' Maud said. 'I remember now where I've seen mesh recently. It was a big exhibition of Aboriginal art and they screen some videos there, too. In one of them a woman picked up a bit of wire mesh—apparently she just found it on the ground, but it looks a bit like barbed wire used to fence a ghetto out—so she picked up this strange piece of material that she found somewhere and in the video she is trying to fold it into a bag. Not quite a dress, but anyway . . . She is turning this rusty piece of wire mesh this way and that—trying to fold in the torn end of it so that she'd have some kind of vessel or a bag. I don't know what they meant by it. You know, the Russian word for a big bag is meshok and it has the same root as mesh. Strange, but it's true.'

'There is also a tulle mesh,' Emma said. 'White tulle is beautiful, I think. You can make a wedding dress out of it, if you like. Remember, Scarlet O'Hara made herself a dress out of a green plush curtain when she was trying to borrow some money from Rhett. I love this dress, the way it looks in the film. Such a beautiful green! But if you could make a dress out of a white tulle curtain, it would be beautiful, too. And it's transparent, remember, you said . . .'

'But seriously, Emma,' Maud interrupted. 'Let's suppose somebody did leave a dress in the room. What means do we have to find out whose dress it is?'

'I think, if it's a newly bought dress, it shouldn't be too difficult. Look, there must be a receipt there in the bag with a dress. Now, if there is a receipt, there are only two options. In the first one, which is the best for us, the girl who bought the dress paid with her bank card. Its number is enough information to find out her name. In the second option, which is not that easy, she paid cash. The day and time when she did it, are on the receipt. We should look then for people who were there, near this shop, on this day and time, among all those people who could have come to this room. Again, if they were near this shop, it is likely that they would use their bank card to withdraw money on the same day. So it means that to find the person, we must look into bank accounts of all people who might possibly have left a bag in the room.'

'Good, but to do all this, we must see a receipt', Emma said. 'Unless we know the day and time when the dress was bought, it's pointless. By the way, did they say it was a new dress? But of course, you are right, it's the only possibility.'

'Let's go there tomorrow,' Maud said.

'We'll say we want to see it, just to make sure it couldn't be mine, and have a good look at the receipt in the bag.'

Emma agreed. The next day, when the friends arrived at the crime scene, the dress had disappeared. They were told so by a secretary sitting in a small room adjacent to the big room where the dress was left.

'It was here on the table just a minute ago,' she said. 'I went out for a couple of minutes, and suddenly, it's gone! I'm afraid, there is nothing to do, we can't find out whose it was now. It's gone.' 'If we are quick and lucky, we can still find it. It was here just a short while ago. The person who took it may be still within these walls. If only we could find her,' Emma said.

'The person who has taken it, if it's her dress, should look like somebody who would buy a transparent dress. She'd be dressed accordingly—let's suppose, in a dress, too. White? Black? Scarlet? What do you think? Look for somebody with a boutique bag in hand.'

'Let's say we've found somebody with a boutique bag in hand,' Emma said. 'How can we know what's inside?'

'We must find a way to make her open it,' Maud said. 'Any way. Of course, we can just push everybody with a boutique bag down the staircase and when they stumble, help them up, and peer inside the bag. But this seems like a crude way to do it. There should be a better way.'

'We can say to any girl with a boutique bag that today, while the bag was in the office, somebody put important documents there, just by mistake. If the bag in question never was in the office, she would just stare and won't understand what we are talking about. But if it was, she'd probably open it and look inside, to see what documents are there.'

Maud and Emma were lucky. The second girl they tried to surprise by claiming there were important documents in her plastic bag didn't just stare. It was a tall girl dressed in a halterneck summer dress and she carried a Kookai bag in her hand. When Emma came close and said somebody put important documents in the bag today, the girl's reaction was immediate. She dropped the bag and ran. Maud and Emma could have run after her, but instead, they picked up the bag, and looked inside. When they planned this approach, the only thing they wanted to know was what kind of girl was the girl who lost her newly bought dress in the room. And, of course, it would be interesting to see what kind of dress it was. Mesh dress sounded intriguing.

What happened was much more than what they expected. They opened the bag, and there was, indeed, a dress. It was black with some decoration, but to say that it was a mesh dress would be a gross exaggeration. A corner of a brown leather-bound book could be seen from under the dress.

'What is this, for God's sake,' Emma whispered, her eyes as big as two shiny saucers, and pulled it out.

'It looks like a diary,' Maud answered. 'An old diary, with this. Let's look what's inside. What, I wonder, has it been doing in this bag?'

The friends opened the diary, hardly able to breathe from excitement. The first page read:

> February the 3rd 1942.
>
> Today was the first day we have arrived to the camp. They placed us in big wooden barracks, approximately one hundred people each. People who have been here for a while say that when the extermination time comes, Nazis burn a shed with all its people. However, it happens almost never because they want to keep the sheds usable.
>
> February the 6th.
>
> The lunch today was not very good. We had cheesecake for dessert and it was soggy.
>
> February the 7th.
>
> Today we've had an all prisoners' assembly for the first time. A number of people spoke about what they learned in prison and how grateful they are. Some of those who spoke received extra dessert. Some got a new job. Amy Fishman has become a baker.

'This diary is quite old,' Maud said. 'It can't possibly belong to the girl who dropped the bag. She is hardly twenty. Somebody else had put it there. But who? And why?'

'Yes,' Emma muttered. 'Assuming that it's a genuine article, it's really strange. It could be her grandmother's diary, I guess. Or another older relative's. But we still need to explain why she put it in the bag with the dress. Maybe she was going somewhere for a couple of days, and took it with her, to read? But what if it's not genuine at all?'

'Anybody could have written something like this,' Maud agreed. 'How can we tell?'

'There are such things as the age of paper and leather, and the ink itself. We can send it off for an analysis and they will tell us how old all these things are. But just theoretically, somebody could have taken a very old leather bound book, that had been lying somewhere in a chest all this time, and written a mock old diary. You know, as if.'

'Also, if it's real,' Maud added, 'It doesn't have to belong to her grandma or any old relative. It could be anybody's. May be she doesn't even know whose it is. Who put it in the bag?'

'Well,' Emma said, 'it looks like we'll have to start with a boring thing like a lab analysis. If it's been written just recently, the book itself can be age old, although, of course, it's highly unlikely, but not the ink. Let's find out how old the ink is.'

The next day Maud and Emma took the leather book to the lab. They wanted to know how old all its parts were: the paper, the leather, and the ink. After all, may be the paper was old, but the book was bound in the new leather recently. The most important part of all was the ink: if it's new, the diary could not be sixty years old.

'Do you want it to be real or not?' Emma asked.

'I don't know,' Maud answered. 'What about you?'

'I'd prefer it to be real,' Emma said. 'What significance does it have if it's a fake? Or somebody's exercise in creative writing? I mean, of course, it can be fascinating, but what real significance does it have?'

They paused and waited in silence until the door of the lab opened and a white-clad assistant appeared.

'I'm afraid I must disappoint you,' she said. 'It is not a genuine article. The leather cover is the only part of the book which is genuine,' the lab assistant said. 'I suspect it comes from an antique shop. As for the paper, it's a bit more complicated. I think it's new paper that has been artificially weathered. There are a few simple ways to make new paper appear old—you can put it in the slow oven for a short time and take out when it starts yellowing. Or just place your paper in the sun in a sheltered or, better still, not so sheltered place, and in two weeks it will appear quite old. It will be crumpled, too, but if you iron it, you will have a smooth bit of old paper. This diary has been assembled from parts of different age and origin: the leather cover is really old, wherever it comes from, the paper they used to write on had been purposefully aged and weathered, and the ink is from a today's shop. This is my conclusion.'

'Not what we expected, uhm?' Emma said, when they stepped outside the building where the lab was located. 'So, it turns out that the diary is a fake. It makes it even harder to explain. It can't be, then, the Kookai girl's grandma's or great-great aunt's diary. Somebody made this strangest of all things I've seen—had bought the leather cover, weathered the paper and wrote the entries, bound it all together, so carefully that it looks real. Who did it? Why?'

'What means do we have to find out,' Maud said again, pensively. 'The bag was lying in the office. That is, until today. For how long? A few days, at least. Anybody or almost anybody could have come in and put this diary thing in the bag. But what could be the motive?'

'I guess,' Maud added, 'it all depends on how far they expected us to go into it. Well, they probably didn't expect *us*—but whoever would find this diary in her dress bag, if anybody does. What could they think? Option one: it's a real thing and it belongs to her grandma. She put it in the bag because she wanted to read it or reread it. Or, just maybe, discuss it at her meeting? In this case, I suppose, it makes her a more interesting person. Charismatic. But we know it's not true. Option two is it's not hers at all, whether it's real or not. Then she must have stolen it. If she's stolen it, she was probably going to sell or auction it. If it was genuine, it could cost lots of money. Option three is that the girl with the bag never even knew that there was a fake diary hidden under her new dress. Somebody had put it there. Why? And who?'

'Maybe, to create a certain impression,' Emma said. 'To make her look suspicious or corrupt? Except, of course, the first option—it's her grandma's—doesn't make her look suspicious, quite the contrary—but it can't be, because it's not real. What if the person who put the diary in the bag was in a hurry to hide it?'

'We can find the person who wrote the diary if we find the ink buyer,' Maud said. 'The ink was bought in a craft shop, most likely. Not many people on the floor, where the bag was found, know where these shops are.'

Of course, there was a chance that the ink belonged to somebody who was not there on the floor. 'Then we'll have to check all her contacts,' Emma sighed. 'Or the ink could belong to somebody who she's never known. Then we'll probably never find this person. But let's check the simplest guess first—see if somebody around has a bottle of ink like the one that was used to write the diary.'

'Let's do a bit of fundraising—we can sell chocolate—and see if we can spot a bottle of ink in any of the rooms,' Maud said.

Maud and Emma did as they said : circled the floor, knocking on each and every door, but, alas, there was absolutely no ink in sight, even remotely similar to that used by the writer of the diary.

'No luck,' Emma said. 'It looks like we'll never know who's written it. After all, why should it be somebody we know and can find easily?'

'Of course, it can be anybody,' Maud said. 'But I feel like the epicentre of this story is here, where it started. It can be a mistake, of course. Let's go and give back all the chocolate we couldn't sell. No luck is no luck.'

The secretary's door was ajar and Maud quickly stepped in. She was leaning over one of the drawers of her desk and there—it couldn't be anything else—was the ink, exactly the same hue as that used to write the diary. Maud and Emma stacked a few chocolate bars on the desk and stepped out.

'Have you seen it?' asked Maud. 'It cannot be anything else. The same hue—dark blue.'

'It would be better to compare the ink in her drawer with the diary,' Emma said. 'But it's unlikely that we'll ever have a chance. Why has she done it?'

'What if she hasn't done it? What if she just keeps a similar ink in her drawer to put us on the wrong track?' Maud objected. 'I'm afraid we'll never know. Unless the girl with the Kookai bag knows more and will tell us. Jane the secretary might have been just playing with an artful imitation—writing an imaginary diary in a leather bound book and then suddenly—bang!—she decided to put it in the girl's bag. Or maybe she has nothing to do with it, but has a similar ink. Who knows? To tell the truth, I don't want to know.'

However, after a bit of poring over it, the friends decided to ask the Kookai girl about it.

'She is a graduate student,' Maud said, 'and probably comes here every week or maybe fortnight to see her supervisor. She can be here next week at the same time, unless they change the appointment time. In this case we'll need an access to her e-mail box to find out. If they change the time over the phone, we'd need to know her mobile number. Let's hope they won't and just wait here next week.'

Next week the Kookai girl appeared on the floor around the same time as the previous week. Emma came close to her, carrying the dress bag. 'I'm sorry we scared you. We didn't expect you to run away. Here is your dress. Did you know there was an old diary hidden under it in the bag?' she said.

'Yes, I know,' the girl said. 'It's my grandma's diary. I had it since I was very young.'

'We had taken it for an analysis,' Emma said. 'It is a fake. The ink used to write a diary is quite new. The paper is new, too, but had been made to appear old.'

'I don't know,' the girl said. 'I remember the book in my childhood, but have never read it until just recently. I was too young.'

Suddenly Emma had an insight.

'Can I have another look at it,' she said. The Kookai girl passed her the diary.

'Look here,' Emma said. 'The ink they used initially is the invisible ink. Probably made from lemon juice or another household acid. People used invisible ink in prisons to hide what they were writing. And then later somebody had written new words over it in normal ink. This new ink is quite visible.'

'I can't believe it,' the girl said. 'It looked like this as long as I can remember it. How can this be?'

'How, indeed,' Maud said. 'May be you can find out?' she continued, encouragingly. 'After all, this interesting object is yours. But it's a fact that they've written one thing over another in it. A fact as factual as a fact can be.'

'I am afraid my insight is wrong,' Emma said. 'It's unlikely that the person who wrote it had lemon juice or even vinegar, if it was written in a camp. Of course, a baker might have had some. Anyway, if you go into it, you must take care lest they announce you to be a witch and burn—it did happen before, remember.'

Barb

As time goes on and my recollections of these events fade, I start thinking more and more often: maybe I should write it down. Why? She was the first and the last Aboriginal person I ever knew well, and she was, indeed, a revelation to me. She called herself an Aboriginal lady. How did I come to know her, is a strange story. But what can I start with? I don't know. Like so many people before me have put it, I will start with just anything, and then piece by piece, line by line, my picture will come alive. It will come together and be whole, like beads, threaded on a line, become a necklace. She loved jewellery, by the way, and so do I. Beads or lines I am planning to make it of—they are English, strange words—shouldn't I be writing it in my own language, at all? But English was the language she spoke, and the language we spoke to each other, and also the language that made it all possible. Because she spoke English, maybe, 'lines' didn't remind her of 'lie', or maybe it did, I will never know. She loved to sing, and sometimes wrote poems under her pictures. She was a lovely person and a great Aboriginal lady.

One.

I met her, because she had paralysis, and I was her carer. It means my job was to come to her house and look after her. I became a carer, because in many years that have gone since the time when I first came to Australia, to study on a scholarship, I've never actually brought myself to look for a job. Or maybe I did, but not quite properly. Anyway, I couldn't bear it for any length of time. It so happened, that I did finish my study—it was clear to me, how to do it—but this was it. I couldn't push myself to do anything else about it, even more so, because I didn't really know, how. So here I was, at eight o'clock on a Saturday morning, some fifteen years later—ringing the bell on her door. The reason I was there was, of course, that I needed money and felt it was a no worse, than any other, if not even better, in some and quite many important respects, way to get it. A man opened the door for me. 'This way, she is in the room,' he said.

I came into the room and saw a black body in bed. Lots of strange things were hanging from the ceiling. 'There are hoists for lifting them,' I remembered. The woman was snoring. I said 'hi' and she blinked her closed eyes a couple of times, lifted her arm and pulled herself to a sitting position. 'Her arms work, it's called paraplegia,' I remembered. Suddenly I thought, once again, about money. This was, indeed, a piece of luck. With a five-hour shift, like this one (and I had the same thing on Sunday!), on a twenty dollars hourly rate, I was going to get a hundred dollars for a day's work. Naturally, I was interested in her liking me.

'What would you like?' I asked.

'A cup of coffee,' she said. 'And, maybe, some breakfast'.

I got out of the room and, on my way to the kitchen, sighed with relief: cooking food was my forte, comparing to operating the strange machinery that was hanging over her head. I made her a coffee and decided on scrambled eggs for her and the man who opened the door for me. I broke the eggs into a frying pan, noticed a packet of 'bush spice' nearby and added it too. Five minutes later, when it was time to give it to them, I found the man in the living room—he was reading clearly old newspapers among empty bottles of grog. 'My name is Krieg, by the way,' he said. 'He must be her partner,' I thought. The formula came to me as a whole, unexpectedly.

Two.

Her name was Barb. She had a twenty-something daughter and a two-year old granddaughter. 'Her daughter will tell me, what to do,' I decided. Something had to be done to Barb after breakfast, but I didn't know, what. But soon found out. Firstly, there was a shower. Like everybody, Barb had to shower. I had to put her into a shower chair, wheel into the shower and help her wash. To do it, I had to put a special thing, made of strong and slippery cloth, a sling, under her, cross its ends between her legs, and hang her in it. It looked like a hammock, hung on four hooks, that were stuck to a metal bar. The hammock and the metal bar could be moved up and down by electric levers. Barb would command, as I was hanging her up, 'higher!', 'more up', and I pressed the 'up' button on the hoist machine. Sometimes, I pressed the wrong one and she screamed 'down!' The buttons were above my head, and if I turned the control panel upside down, the 'up' arrow would become 'down' and 'down'—'up'. 'What can this be a symbol of?' I thought each time, when I accidentally hit a wrong button. Down under? Something else? There was little time to think it over, but I wanted to find something. 'A bit to the left,' Barb would say, as I was lowering her hammock into the chair. Then I would get her up again, and, when she was going down, press her to the left, to help her fit into the chair. All in all, it was fun and made me feel a highly responsible person.

Three.

Perhaps, Barb didn't think that these hammock flights over her chair were much fun, because one day, when I came to her place on a Saturday morning, I found, that she broke her leg and had to be taken to hospital. 'She was trying to walk,' Krieg explained to me. 'She couldn't accept, that she cannot'. On the way back, I was trying to decide, if this could be, in any sense, my fault. Was I too inattentive? Or maybe, too protective? Or, maybe, just too complacently satisfied of being able to walk? I couldn't decide, if any of this was true, but, of course, I wanted her to come back, as soon as possible.

Four.

It was a hot spring in November, when Barb came back. Now, when I'd come in, she would be still asleep. Maybe, she was tired from an endless procession of people, coming to look after her. Eighteen or twenty hours of her day were 'covered'. Or, maybe, the time of my morning appearance was too early for her. Both of us had to wait, anyway, until my work partner would come in, an hour later, at nine. Since Barb broke her leg, nobody was allowed to transfer her, as they call it, that is, to lift her into the chair, single handedly. I would come at eight and sit at her kitchen table, doing crosswords or reading a book, while Barb had another hour of sleep. There was no hurry, five hours was sure plenty of time. 'Why does it start so early?' I wondered sometimes, feeling almost impatient to start. But I was too sleepy myself to contemplate this question for a long time.

Five.

My work partner's name was Rosa. She was a student nurse, and a very serious girl. As we put Barb into her hammock, and the TV was on, we watched it and chatted—about everything. Who we like, who is beautiful, who sings well, and who doesn't. Hers, and mine, and Barb's childhood.

It turned out, as we were hanging her up, that Barb never really knew her parents. She was from the stolen generation and adopted. Somehow she believed, and I never found out, if it was true, that her adoptive father was German. She knew her sister, but had lost her long ago. She also had a lot of brothers by adoption, in her father's family, back there in Queensland. How did she get adopted? She never answered this question, nor many other I asked about her childhood. Was it because she felt, after she asked some questions herself, that I was well protected, and secure, and actually happy most of the time, while she at the same age was . . . what? She never really complained and left me wondering. She couldn't read fluently and hardly ever did it for herself—was it because she didn't go to school? She drank so much—when did she start? There were strange little things, that impressed me: she loved pumpkin soup, but didn't know, how to make it. Was it, because there was no pumpkin around, when she was a child? How could it be? What was she actually doing, most of the time, before she had her children? And when was it? I couldn't tell, how old she was, as is often the case with people who live a life like that, but she seemed quite young. Perhaps, under forty. 'No, this is, probably, not true,' I thought, remembering, that her granddaughter is two. How did it happen, that she had them so early? The only thing she would tell about it, was that the father of her children was Spanish. So was Rosa, my partner in transferring Barb into her chair.

Six.

'You like Rosa, don't you?' Barb asked once, after Rosa had gone and left me to wheel Barb in her shower chair out of the shower, and then put her back into her hammock, onto the bed, into her clothes and, at last, into her usual motorised chair, that she used during the day. 'Yes,' I said. 'Sure'. Rosa was pretty. These morning conversations above the devices, used to move and wash Barb, could be the closest I ever came to friendship in Australia. Well, perhaps, not. Of course I knew some people who came from the same city, as I did. Leaving this aside, of course, I liked talking to Rosa, too. But did I like her? I wasn't sure. There was so much in her, that I couldn't like. I found her judgements judgemental. And her seriousness about her mortgage a bit over the top (I can't even think of taking one). The question I contemplate at times is 'Who am I more like? Barb with her crazy nonchalance or Rosa with her meticulousness?'

In fact, I feel I'm not like any of them. It's a question that makes no sense to me. You can't compare and it is, actually, hard to really like a flower that grew up in a different soil. How much does it have to do with what happened to Barb? I'm not sure, but, I suspect, it's a lot.

Seven.

Barb and I both like the same simple pleasures. A cuppa with something sweet, probably, rates first among them. Or an expedition to a garage sale nearby. Or window-shopping for jewellery. Once Barb is washed in the morning, we often go somewhere, not very far away, to buy a coffee in a coffee shop, and after Barb's resources have been considerably diminished by this, she wants to go to a garage sale. and I don't mind it, either. As I'm watching her to devour a custard pastry, that leaves her hands and face sticky, and thinking about, maybe, getting the same one for myself, I am trying to decide, why here, in this particular point, we are so alike. Generally, I don't feel very much like her. When she lived (where? I am not sure; maybe in a dormitory, or was it her adopted home?) and, probably, felt deprived of most of the things she likes now, I was at home, having music lessons. The only slightly disturbing thing about this thought is, that it would never occur to me, if I wasn't standing there, watching her eat. But why is it, that now I want it too? I cannot decide, whether it's because food was often not quite what you'd call in abundance, when I was growing up, or is it simply because right now I'm her shadow? Or is there, maybe, a connection between the two? But why?

Eight.

My favourite person in Barb's household is her two-year old granddaughter Lizzie. Usually, two or three hours is enough time to finish all my tasks with Barb, and when they are finished, I would sit somewhere in a remote corner of Barb's house and play with Lizzie. She doesn't attend anything a two-year old child could attend, and her grandma's carers are her main connection to the outside world.

One thing, she particularly likes about the morning shower ritual of her grandmother, is using her sling as a swing. Once Barb is in the sling and ready to be lifted above her bed, Lizzie would climb onto her leg or belly and sit there, waiting for Barb to go higher. Up in the air she screams something joyful, like 'Up we go! Hooray!' and would climb down on the ground, only after Barb is lowered into her chair. It makes the whole task a little bit more difficult for the person who does it, but provides lots of entertainment to Lizzie. Sometimes, I wonder, how she sees it all. I seems obvious, that none of the things, related to her grandmother's illness, has the same sinister meaning for her, as they do for relative outsiders, like Rosa and me. But she seems so normal and wholesome in everything else. I don't know, who her father is, it seems, it's a bit of a family secret, but I love her hair: lots of shiny black curls that I can see, are the same colour as Barb's, when Lizzie is sitting on her belly, waiting to go up in the sling.

Nine.

Barb, I found out, believed in magic and was very serious about it. She even thinks, that she herself has supernatural powers. Sometimes, she wants to cast a spell and starts whispering. I don't know, what she says, because she likes to be alone, when she does it. Once, however, she started a conversation on voices, that talk to her, and I learned, that they belong to spirits, that she's known for a long time. It seems, that magic and conversations to spirits are something like a honourable tradition to Barb, that she feels she is bound to uphold, simply because she is Aboriginal. It seems, she's seen many other people doing it, and, perhaps, they were good ones to her. But in her present context, her magic beliefs are hardly shared by anyone. Even I tell her, that spirits she talks to should better be sober. Perhaps, I would learn more on them, if I didn't.

Beliefs, which are not shared by anyone, are called schizophrenia, and Barb, instead of a sacred place for doing magical things, or whatever it has to be, has a locked cupboard in her house where her nurses regularly put her schizophrenia medication for a week.

The cupboard is locked, the nurse told me, because otherwise Lizzie could reach and swallow the medication. It is my responsibility to open the cupboard in the morning, make sure, that Lizzie doesn't touch anything, and give a tablet to Barb. In her present context, she is crazy with her spells, but would she be seen in the same way, if she lived somewhere out there, among other magicians? Is craziness always just a matter of context and location? Or the number of people, who could, possibly, believe in the same thing? Or their trustworthiness? Who could be such a trustworthy person among all those who deal with Barb everyday?

Ten.

Barb is a chain smoker. She starts her day with a cigarette, and if there are none, because there is no money to buy them, she is grumpy. Sometimes, she rolls some herself, using pre-cut paper and tobacco, but she prefers those sold in packets. It seems, that a cigarette pack has a feel of luxury to her: it's not even the taste or smell of cigarettes, that she is addicted to, it's a smooth silky feel of a shop-bought packet in her hand. Barb has asthma, but nobody is brave enough (or just cares enough about her?), to tell her to stop. One of her main sources of cigs, as she tenderly calls them, are, of course, her carers. Almost everybody smokes and brings some for Barb. In fact, I haven't smoked a cigarette since my student days, but just to keep Barb company . . . why not? I also hope, that it will make her like me better, and I will keep these fantastically good hours longer. But it doesn't, really. Actually, she much prefers to borrow ten dollars from a person and then use it, mostly for cigarettes, and, sometimes, for beer and the like, after they've gone, but it's rarely possible.

Eleven.

Another thing that Barb likes almost as much, as cigarettes, is clothes. When she became paralysed about ten years ago, it made her want to look beautiful more, than before. Something tells me, that she couldn't be indifferent to it, when she was in good health either, although I couldn't explain clearly, what it is. She is one of these women who are sure of themselves, because they look good. And, I think, she did look good, before she got run over by a car and ended up in a wheelchair. Now she sees clothes, as her main tool of achieving good looks, and she's got piles of them. Literally mountains. She is especially fond of silk blouses, and before she decides on one in the morning, she can try three or four. Like a smart packet of cigarettes, and maybe even more, silk blouses mean to her, that she is not poor. She is, but I try to concentrate on other things, when I see her making an effort to choose the right shiny number for the day.

Twelve.

Barb has severe burns on both her feet. I'm not sure, how she got them, but they make looking after her body an even more complicated enterprise, than it would be otherwise. A nurse comes to see her two or three times a week, and changes the dressing on the wounds, and after she's left, I try to bandage Barb's ankles with long elastic bandages, exactly the way it was before. Barb's legs are paralysed, and the circulation around the feet is limited, and everything heals very slowly, if at all. Barb says, she got these wounds, when she fell asleep with her naked feet turned towards the heater. She didn't feel any pain, since her feet are paralysed. Was she drunk too? It seems obvious, that she was. As usual with Barb, one bad thing seems to lead to another, in an almost fatal, inevitable way. When did it start? One cannot see the starting point now, but I don't feel, as absurd as it sounds, that it's Barb's fault, if she sleeps, heavily drunk, while her feet are burning on the heater. I feel, it must be somebody else's.

Thirteen.

Barb has two children, a son and a daughter, close in age, somewhere in their early twenties. Neither of them was working nor studying at the time, when I was Barb's carer, but I like them both. The first thing you notice about both is, perhaps, their beauty. Both Barb's children are extremely beautiful. And very musical, and often sing songs, walking around the house. When they don't sing, they mostly scream, as both get easily irritated, and quarrel a lot with each other. Outside the family, they don't seem to have many people they'd know or be close with. Somehow, they project a strange feeling of living on an uninhabited island, being strangers to what's around, although I know, that they spent, apparently, all their childhood in this city. Anyway, whatever the reason, it's something I can understand, and I find them intelligent.

Fourteen.

Barb doesn't know, how to use an ATM, and she doesn't have a bank card. When she needs to withdraw some money from her pension, she goes to the post office, and tells the shop lady, that she needs to have money withdrawn. When she first told me this is the way she does it, I wouldn't believe her, but it is true. Often we go to the post together: I pay my bills, which I only remember, when I'm with her, I don't know why, and she asks the lady to withdraw for her. I wonder, if the way Barb handles her money affairs, if one can call it so, means, that she was once found unfit to do it any other way. I could ask, but it doesn't look like she knows herself.

Fifteen.

Barb likes to draw and often buys coloured pencils and paints. She draws typical naïve pictures with animals and flowers, sometimes with Aboriginal motives and dots. I really like some of them, although, of course, they are really simple. Are they worse, however, than some other stuff, that can be branded as Aboriginal and successfully sold? I'm not sure all of them are, and there is no way to check my unprofessional opinion, because she's never tried to show them to anybody, who'd know. Or, rather, she never had a chance to do it. She didn't have a chance to work on her painting skills, either. Sometimes, she starts planning and says, she wants to attend a painting class. But, realistically, it's not possible. A special taxi to any, even the closest venue, she could choose, would cost more, than she can afford, let alone the cost of a class. It cannot be done on her pension. 'How much would it change for her?' I wonder. 'Maybe, not much. After all, they are not such good pictures'.

Barb likes to sing, too. She has a strong voice, that sounds like something out of the ordinary to me, unlike her painting, and she is musical. But, it seems, she doesn't know the first thing about music, because nobody's ever told her. Perhaps, it's too late now: a person who has gangrene on both her feet should be thinking about it, not about painting classes.

Sixteen.

What is the last thing, that should be said about Barb? Perhaps, it is that she fell a victim to being one of her generation. And that I did, too. If I wasn't born at the time, when I was, and wasn't the age I was, when the Soviet Union fell apart, and life had changed so much, I would never meet Barb. Perhaps, I could say, that we both belong to 'lost' or 'stolen' generations, only in a slightly different way. But it doesn't seem, in the least, true. What happened to me and other people, like me, is immeasurably better, than what happened to Barb. Was it accidental, or was there a reason for it? I will never know, because one lifetime is just not enough time to see.

Trial and error.

One day Ed felt he was tired of going from one person he cared for to another, for a job. He wanted to look for a change and hoped for the best. After a short search, he succeeded. His new post was called, like the previous one, 'care attendant', and involved, well, care provided to people who, presumably, needed it. That is, around the same amount of showing how to shower, and other things that come with it. However, one thing was definitely better: his new post didn't involve constant commuting between people in need of care, since they were all gathered under the same roof, called a residential housing. He would spend three to four hours in a row there at once, which was clearly a bonus, compared to the previous situation, when he only had an hour or so of paid time to spend in one place. To compensate for this, he would be paid a bit less for an hour. This, of course, was not the best possible thing, but Ed was prepared to give it a try anyway. It was a change, after all.

The first few days were devoted, as usual, to what was called orientation. A group of very diverse people gathered in the big hall of what was now Ed's new place of work—it was called, perhaps, by someone sentimental, a long time ago,— villa Elsa. They had to sit through five days of lecturing, as diverse and disorderly, as their clothes and shoes were. It included a first aid course and some information on epilepsy, previously unknown to Ed, despite the fact that he was an epileptic himself, fire extinguishing exercises and tips on how to handle rotten meat, when you are quickly organising a meal for four to five people. Ed, who always liked to watch people talk, sat through all of it with vivid pleasure. He even got a chance to hold a big red fire extinguishing hose, but missed the target and instead covered the arm of one of the teachers with white foam. The undoubtedly useful thing, he found, was bits and pieces he was told on epilepsy: he felt proud he had an access to the information unavailable to just anybody. 'Plenty of children and even babies, it turns out, have it, without their parent ever suspecting it. Unless, of course, they have a chance to attend a useful course like this one,' Ed thought.

Finally, the first five days were over. His new boss was a plump middle-aged woman with kind grey eyes and an encouraging habit of looking deep into your eyes, as she spoke. Her name was Betty and she was about Ed's age, although she seemed a bit older. 'Is she married,' he wondered with fear, knowing from his previous experience, how much her general disposition and attitude are likely to depend on it. He soon found out that she wasn't, but at least she wasn't childless. 'It makes it easier,' he decided, but was mistaken.

He felt from the beginning, that Betty didn't like him, although he couldn't exactly tell why, and what does it have to do with her not being married. He himself was, but didn't think it affected his attitude to her. 'Maybe this is the very thing that makes her angry,' he suddenly thought. 'The fact that I can't see her as a woman. Can anybody else, I wonder? Well, I suppose, it's none of my business.' Although Ed could, by no means, exclude the possibility that somebody else could find Betty attractive, he himself couldn't imagine it. In this case, he soon realized, he'd better not think of it at all. 'She gets along quite well with plenty of other people,' Ed noticed. 'What is it, then? Is it me? Is it them?' By 'them' he meant the people who lived in the residential house, where he worked. The residents, as they called them. There were four residents, all of them, he was told, intellectually disabled. Actually, there were five. The fifth one, Andrew, was blind, and Betty especially emphasized, when she explained to Ed all he had to know about it, that Andrew was, of course, intellectually disabled too, although he himself would deny it. 'It's not me,' Ed decided as he recalled in every detail this conversation with Betty. 'It must be them. She sees them . . . well, how? In a different light, maybe.' He wasn't quite sure himself, in what light he saw them. Mostly because he didn't see too many people like this before, and they didn't seem to belong anywhere to him. Nor fall into any reasonable category. Every each one of them seemed a person like no other to Ed, and this was the only thing they had in common. It almost reconciled Ed with his new position. 'Almost' because he wasn't sure that what he was doing wasn't wrong. He felt that people he was considered to be looking after were locked up there. It was hard to imagine, that any of them would choose to stay in the place permanently by themselves. On the other hand, the commonsense, that Ed knew he had not enough of, told him they were not qualified to choose. Although not qualified to do so, they were, he knew, as a result of somebody else's decision. But what choice there could be for people who couldn't look after themselves? But, again, couldn't they, really? Or were they, along with everybody else, just convinced that they couldn't? Ed was a firm believer in the powers of convincing. And also in the fact, that most of it is done for a purpose, although one may not see clearly, what it is.

One person, however, of those five Ed met recently, seemed clearly happy of her position. Ashley was about thirty or a bit older, and needed a frame to walk. One of her feet was deformed, Ed noticed, when he first had to help her to put on her orthopaedic shoes. She was clumsy, and couldn't reach her foot herself. In fact, her motor skills were so bad, that it was hard to say, what the girl was like. Either because it was hard for her to articulate, or just because she was shy, or maybe because one thing naturally led to another, she said very little. In the beginning, Ed had to ask her to repeat everything she said, twice. 'Is she that bad,' he wondered, 'or is it my foreign ear? Or does she, too, have an accent, by any chance?' Looking at Ashley, he suspected that she might, but didn't dare to ask. There was an air of reserved dignity, bordering on suppressed anger, about her that made Ed shy. Despite having a frame, she worked somewhere in the factory. 'Do you know,' Betty told him one day, 'Ashley has a fiancé?' Before Ed could fully overcome his surprise, she added, 'She met him at work. They are trying to organize a move now, so as to reside in the same house. But, personally, I object. Not here. I don't understand it: if you see somebody at work everyday, why would you want to see them at home?' 'Aren't they supposed to have a choice?' Ed asked, but she didn't answer.

One of the things Ed did regularly, as part of his morning duty, was shaving residents, men and, strangely, women. To be precise, he had to shave the face of one of three women in the house. Lily was an extremely thin and pale creature who was so timid, Ed himself felt like a solid fortress of confidence. Something must have been severely wrong with her hormones, but instead of being corrected, they just shaved her. That is, Ed was paid a bit less, than in his previous job, to do it. It might have been better, if Lily, who was quite good with her hands, tried to dress pretty and was proud of her work achievements, documented by certificates displayed on the wall of her room, did it herself, but somebody decided she shouldn't. Or, maybe, she really couldn't, Ed had no way to tell, although it was a bit hard to imagine it, looking at how fast and smart she is with little picture puzzle bits, she joined together in a picture on the floor of her room, trying to delay the shaving moment for as long as possible. Ed would come to her room every morning around nine o'clock, and waiting for her to finish dressing, combing her hair and doing her puzzles, read whatever he could find to read on the wall, and uttered something encouraging now and then. Ashley's entire work history was on the wall, which was, he found, a bit longer, than his own. He read about what he thought might have been the better part of her life—saying things clearly aloud, for her. 'Certificate one in horticulture,' he read, 'your hair looks really good now. Certificate two in retail work. Did you work in a shop? Did you like it? I don't think I would cope with work at the counter. You must be really brave.' No matter how many encouraging things he said, she was extremely slow to make her way to the bathroom sink, where the shaving itself happened. Maybe, Ed thought later, she anticipated with a kind of sharpened intuition, some people acquire in a position like this ('like what?' he asked himself, 'when they are repeatedly humiliated? Depend on somebody's whim? Or just never quite know what to expect next?' He settled on the last one and was right), she must have anticipated what happened one day. There was no shaving foam in the tube. Maybe, it just run out, or maybe, somebody's taken it. In fact, there was no reason to believe it was taken, except that it was full the day before, he remembered. It should have stopped him, but it didn't. Why? He couldn't tell. It didn't make any sense at all, but just happened. He felt, he thought, as pushed, as Lily, to do it, and there was nobody around, whom he could ask if he could skip it. Did he need to ask? He decided he'd manage anyway, and cut Lily's small and slightly shrunken face twice, while he was doing it. He might have felt guilty, but didn't. As often, he tried to blame somebody else. Who thought up this terrible routine of shaving a thirty something woman, able to do it by herself, if absolutely necessary, in the first place? Who's taken the foam? He felt like he was just a tool in somebody else's hand, a razor in this particular case. Whose hand? He couldn't tell.

The only thing that's happened during his time at the villa, that he was happy of, was that he managed to convince Betty, against all odds, that one of the older women didn't wet her pants at night. She sneezed hard in the morning, as she nursed her asthma, waiting for the only bathroom to be free, but somehow Betty chose to believe not this version, but another one: the woman was so stupid, she didn't know she had to use the bathroom at night. But Ed convinced her otherwise.

The day finally came, not quite unexpectedly for Ed, since it was hinted upon before he even started, when he was fired. He didn't get along with Betty, and it was obvious to them both. He was paid a four weeks wages at once and felt entirely happy. Thinking of people left in the house he felt like he was flying: he was free. He wondered, if they are going to be better off without him, but not very hard.

All connected

'Would you mind if I joined the anarchist party?' Ed asked his wife Ellie one day.

Ellie was so surprised that for a moment or two she couldn't find what to say.

'You? Join the party? Why?' she said at last.

'I don't know,' Ed said. 'I just happened to read a bit about them lately and I was thinking that it would, you know, express precisely what I was thinking. But if you mind . . .'

'You must be going crazy,' Ellie said. 'How can joining a party express what you've been thinking? What is it, anyway? Haven't you had enough of parties and stuff in your previous life, I mean, before you moved here from overseas?'

'I was never a party animal, even in my previous life,' Ed said. 'Although, of course, I was a bit more social than I am now. But seriously, if I joined now, it would be quite a different matter, because it wouldn't be forced. I just feel like it, it's hard to explain why.'

'But did you think about me?' Ellie asked. 'I mean, how it would affect my job. It's something only people like you can afford. The anarchism. But if you had a decent job . . .'

'So you don't like them or do you think you can't make a move like that without jeopardising, you know . . .' Ed asked. 'Or do you think it's the same thing, by any chance? I am sure you must be wrong about the dangers of being involved. And even if you are right, how on Earth can we be sure if it's true, unless we try?'

'We?' Ellie said.

'How can you ask me for a sacrifice like that?' Ed said.

'What sacrifice?'

'To sacrifice what I've been thinking and not to join them, I mean.'

'It wouldn't be a sacrifice just for my sake,' Ellie noted. 'It could help you, too. Don't you see it?'

'No,' Ed said firmly. 'No sacrifice would help in my case. And anyway, I'm above this kind of bargaining. I mean, you know how the old joke goes: to bargain, you need somebody to make you an offer, and if nobody does, you can be well above it.'

'Ok.' Ellie said. 'I think I've fallen out of love with . . . with . . . with this kind of humour. I find it strange that you didn't. And anyway, I don't see how you can find it attractive.'

'What, anarchists?'

'Yes.'

'I don't know how to explain,' Ed said. 'I think the explanation, for me, lies in a number of pictures. You know, like snapshots that you store in your memory. Each one is like a little piece of a puzzle, if you want. But they are not really connected. Not in any real sense, I mean.'

'You can connect them yourself,' Ellie said. 'Everything is connected with everything, if you look well. Do you know why England has such a strong navy?'

'No. Why?'

'Because there are so many spinsters there. Or, maybe, just women. They love cats, cats eat rats, consequently rats cannot damage food supplies on ships and ship crews thrive on lots of good food.'

'I see. But how do cats get on board of ships?'

'It's a good question.' Ellie looked pensive. 'I don't know. You get the idea, anyway. I mean, of paramount connection.'

'I can tell you about my anarchist feelings in this manner. Just one little snapshot after another. I can even draw this kind of 'cats to royal navy' connections between them, if you like.'

'Before I tell you about my first snapshot, I want to say something else,' Ed said, sitting down at the kitchen table. 'You know what made me feel the way I'm feeling now?'

'No. What?'

'It was when I realized that essentially they are all the same.'

'Who?'

'States and systems, of course.'

'It's not true,' Ellie said. 'Isn't the whole human history about how one phase was different from another? People kill each other for change, but you think it's all the same thing, essentially.'

'Whatever,' Ed said. 'They may kill each other and think the change will bring happiness or, at least, relief, but their relationship to what they get in the end is, essentially, the same.'

'In what way?'

'It you cannot stand it all with one regime, it's very likely that you won't like it with another.'

'Why? If they are so different?'

'I don't know. But I do know that there are people who are always opposed to the, what do you call it, mainstream ideas? I don't know. Whatever. And, on the other hand, those who always believe in them, and act accordingly, whatever mainstream means at the moment.'

'If people always find themselves in the opposition camp, it just shows that they are maladjusted,' Ellie said. 'If there are such people, anyway.'

'Perhaps,' Ed said. 'But what about those who always get along with the system, whatever it is? Are they well adjusted?'

'What do you mean 'always'? How is it possible?'

'Why not? It happens all the time. I'll tell you later who I think they are. Somehow I don't want to say it now. I get too emotional, you know.'

'What about what did you call it? . . . Snapshots? Did you say you can explain what you mean if I could just see what you have?'

'Yeah. Kind of. I'll give you my first picture now.'

'I'll give you my first picture now,' Ed said. 'I hope you'll see why I am thinking the way I am now. I saw a girl the other day. At a bus stop.'

'Uh,' Ellie said. 'Just a girl? The way you started your story, I thought it would be something more dangerous than just a girl. Threatening in a way. A fateful revelation, maybe?'

'For me she was,' Ed said. 'Or could be, if I was a woman. I mean, if I was somebody who could be in her place.'

'What was she like?' Ellie asked, at last, a bit reluctantly.

'What was she like . . .' Ed prolonged the last 'al' in 'like' as he was trying to formulate his impression. 'She was . . . was like the opposite of everything I like. Sorry,' he added.

'Goodness,' Ellie was getting impatient. 'You are taking ages. I still don't get it. You've seen a girl and she makes you think, you are saying, anarchist thoughts. Did I get this bit right? Can you tell me why?'

'Yeah,' Ed said. 'I can. But, you see, I am embarrassed. But, if you insist . . . She was . . . was such a product of the way we live.'

'What do you mean? How?'

'She was dressed for the office, straight skirt and a white blouse, and there was a lot of foundation cream on her face, although she was quite young. Maybe twenty six or seven. She had a strange look, I thought. It was at once like . . . like the look of somebody who is scared and is going to run away, and a bit aggressive, too, like she can always turn around and snap. She was holding two lunch boxes. There were sandwiches in one of them. And while she was waiting for the bus next to me, she opened another and started to eat wasabi peas from it.'

'So?' Ellie said. 'I still don't get it. You didn't like her lunch, I see. Nor her make-up. And it makes you to conclude that . . . What does it have to do with the system? The things you were saying before, I mean.'

'I don't know how to tell you,' Ed said. 'One of the thoughts that I was thinking, as I watched her, was that she obviously wants to be attractive and trying hard, too. But she wasn't. Not to me, anyway. And I thought that if she didn't have this 'I am just in an awful hurry for my starting time' look on her face, then, maybe, she would be. Especially, if she had different clothes on.'

'Even if you're right, which I doubt, what does it have to do with everything else? The system and all?'

'It's the system that makes girls like her unattractive. Doesn't it prove it's all wrong?' Ed said.

'I say it's a fresh approach,' Ellie said. 'But you are just heavily biased. Because it's not what you've chosen for yourself, you can't like it. We rarely like the look of people whose lifestyle is very different. I think it's natural.'

'It seems to explain it, in a way. But I think, if you'd see for yourself that empty gaze of hers . . . Or her stilted gait because of high heels. There is absolutely nothing natural about this kind of human being. I mean, just ask yourself, what is it she is trying to achieve and what it's necessary for? What's the purpose of her being in such a hurry in the morning?'

'I am sure she does something that makes sense,' Ellie said. 'I do, at least. Helps somebody, perhaps. I do, in a way. And you can't just dismiss people because you find them purposeless. What's your own purpose, anyway? Or does her two lunchboxes and too much make-up matter more to you than abstract things like a purpose?'

'Yeah, kind of,' Ed said. 'I can't explain any better. It's not the question of purpose, although I did think that her stretched daily routine better be for a purpose. Apart from that . . . I thought, she must be so unkind. So bitchy.'

'Why?'

'I just know it.'

'This is crazy,' Ellie said. 'Can't you see that you can't say 'I don't like people because of the way they look?' Or because their lunch is different?'

'I know,' Ed said. 'But I can't help it. I'm trying, however, it's already something. Don't you think that everybody can and does dislike people because of the way they look? And sound?'

'What's another piece of your puzzle?' Ellie asked, after a pause.

'Another? I'm not sure which one to choose as the next one. Maybe this one. You know what I've seen the other day?'

'You always start like this. One could think that you've seen a monster with five heads or something even more scary. And then it turns out it was a girl.'

'What's so scary about five heads unless they think like one? Seriously, you know what it was?'

'What?'

'An ad. And you know what was in it?'

'No. What?'

'A white goat. Looking mild and sheepish. From my human point of view, rather a woman than a man, and in a hat, too. It made me thinking.'

'Thinking what?'

'Well, obvious thoughts like 'what kind of goat is it, is it meant to be a scapegoat?'

'Why a scapegoat?'

'Well, if it's not meant to be a scapegoat, then what is it meant to be? It has to mean something, or does it not?'

'I don't know. But if it is a scapegoat, who do you think they mean it is?'

'I don't know. What do you think they mean?'

'I don't know either. I'm not sure I've even seen it.'

'Have you noticed that 'goat' sounds like the last words in 'having a go at'?

'But it doesn't mean it's meant to be it, does it?'

'No. Another thing I've noticed about the goat is that it's supposed to be a business-minded goat.'

'Why?'

'There were two bubbles above its head and a word in each one. Two words: 'bargain' and 'reckon.' I was trying to work out what it means, and the only way I can understand it is: goats, whatever they might be, are bargain hunters. Or, maybe, the other way round: we've had enough bargain hunters here and it's time they become goats.'

'Hmm.' Ellie thought for a minute and asked: 'is this story related to your other one?'

'Well,' Ed said. 'In a sad and obvious way. I think the connection is that dislike is always mutual and it's impossible to say who started it first. I identify with the goat side.'

'You? Why?'

'Well, it's obvious, too. I speak with an accent that you'd never call anything but thick as a winter coat. I never or almost never had a decent job here. And you know what, when the other day I came for a staff assembly for people like me, those who work with disabled, at the head office, they simply stood us up. It was cancelled. So, you see, I was thinking: 'Who am I if not a goat?''

'Well, it's too much,' Ellie said. 'You are yourself. You are my husband.'

'I mean, who am I, allegorically speaking?'

'Ah.'

'You know what,' Ed continued, 'as I was going all the way back from this cancelled meeting, I was thinking, 'strange, but I'm not even angry. In fact, I'm feeling very good. Why do you think it was like this to me?'

'I don't know. Why?'

'Because I don't take seriously any of this. It's just a way to earn some cash. Not enough, unfortunately. You know why? Because the woman it depends on looks like the one I told you about before. Not precisely, of course. Just the same type. But it's good they stood me up, because it means that I am a goat, after all, and it explains everything.' After a short pause, Ed added, 'I think they'd hate me even more, if they knew that I am not angry.'

'Why? Do you think they do it to make you angry? You are exaggerating and very much so.'

'If they don't mean to make me angry, then why? You tell me, why?'

'I think they don't care,' Ellie said.

'Maybe you're right here. They don't. But you see, to me, it's all related: the way they stood us up—the goat—the girl with two lunchboxes I told you before. Just think about the food in those lunchboxes, will you? It can't taste good, can it? It's a matter of taste, of course, but when you come to think of it . . .'

'This is why they dislike you,' Ellie said. 'Because you're so sure the food in their lunchboxes is rubbish.'

'I think,' Ed said, 'it's the other way round. Before I met the first girl like that, I had never asked myself what the food in her lunchbox would be like, and the first one disliked me immediately. Who knows where the start is? But, personally, I believe that it's the more what d'you call it? . . . well-adjusted, is it? side who is responsible. It's the more active side, too.'

'What d'you mean?'

'I mean that, if this girl I told you about and I dislike each other, because she reminds me of somebody, it's her who is responsible. I'm just too meek a person to start anything like this. Or should I say I was?'

'It's so vague it's nearly absurd,' Ellie said and added 'Your situation is nearly desperate, I see. If there is such a thing as nearly desperate. But tell me, what can you do that would be sellable?'

'I think I can do . . . well, a few things,' Ed said, solemnly.

'What are they?'

'Don't you know?'

'I do, but I'm not sure what you mean.'

'Well, the first thing that I think I can do really well is choosing clothes.'

'Pardon me?'

'Yes. Choosing clothes. Not that I actually do it, of course. I don't buy many clothes because it's not the kind of thing I prefer to spend on. There are more important things than that, and anyway, I can't be bothered. But I know I can do it well. Quite well, in fact.'

'How do you know?'

'I just know. If you can do something, you know you can, whether you do it or not. Don't you agree?'

'Is the reverse true too?' Ellie asked. 'If you can't do something, you know it too, whether or not you are doing it.'

'Wouldn't you know better?'

'But seriously, why do you think you are a clothes expert at heart?'

'I can just feel it. I always feel it, when I do have to choose something for myself.'

'Then you should have been a buyer for some store,' Ellie said. 'If your self-assessment is true, of course. Do you think you would enjoy it, if you did it on a large scale?'

'How can I tell? If I'm not even doing it on a small scale? I know nothing about stores and the way they do it. The point is: I know I can do it well. One thing I'd like to choose is a new look for girls like the one I told you about. But maybe it just can't be done, without changing everything else. Has it ever occurred to you, by the way, why so much of the so-called business wear is black or dark in colour?'

'No. Why?'

'Because people who wear it, used to write with ink and had to wear something that wouldn't get instantly stained. Everything is logical, you see.'

'Ah.'

'Seriously, the important thing is, I think, whether you like the same things, as most people do, and have a similar taste.'

'I'm sure you don't,' Ellie said.

'You always are.'

'What was the next thing you can do well?'

'The next thing? The next thing . . . Which one should I pick up . . . You are discouraging me.'

'Am I? Why?'

'The next thing I can do well . . . can't you tell me, maybe? It would make my position stronger.'

'I know you are going to say you can teach.'

'Don't you agree?'

'I do. It's hard for me to compare you with somebody else, because . . . I don't know why . . .'

'I think I can teach almost anybody things I can do or know myself.'

'What things would that be? Choosing clothes?'

'No. You wicked creature. I mean, elementary things to very young children. Or a language like my own. Or, maybe, French.'

'Why don't you do it then?'

'You know why. It's impossible, unless you have a whole lot of papers I don't. But I think it just doesn't make any sense. Look at all those people who do have them. You'd expect them to be really good at what they are doing, right? But you know and everybody does it's not always true.'

'Yea-ah,' Ellie said, reluctantly. 'Kind of. Sometimes. Why do you think it happens? I've always thought experience is the key to success in everything. And definitely it is, if you have to fight resistance of a bunch of kids cramming things like algebra into their heads.'

'Maybe experience is important, but it's not the only thing. You've got to really want them to get what you're saying. I mean, if you're to get anywhere at all with it. It's not necessarily people who have loads of experience who are passionate about what they're doing. They get tired, it's natural. Or they just don't want to succeed. I mean, they don't really want everybody they deal with to understand what they have to say. I don't know if this part is natural, but I've seen it so many times.'

'It's the same everywhere. You can't like everybody.'

'You can't like everybody, but, if you just don't want a kid to understand, because you don't like him, it's different. And it's not the same everywhere. The more money people who are legally allowed to do it make, the thicker is the stack of papers, and all kinds of certificates and diplomas you have to have, before you are allowed to do it, too. On the other hand, in some parts of the world teaching, let's say, at school, is not well paid for at all, and as a consequence some people who really want to do it, and it's their only credentials, get in. And quite often they are not the worst ones at all. It's not as strictly regulated, because there is no real money in it.'

'Are you saying they shouldn't be paid that much and then it'll get better?'

'No, of course not. I just don't see why it's such a strict rules system. Somebody should benefit from it, but who is it?'

At this point Ed and Ellie's conversation was interrupted by somebody knocking on the door. Ed got up to open it and asked Ellie 'Who do you think it is?' She shrugged her shoulders 'I'm not expecting anyone.'

Ed opened the door and, at first, didn't recognize the person who fell in. In was their neighbour Peter, almost completely covered by soap foam and fully naked.

Ellie was able to speak first. 'What happened?' she breathed out. 'My house is on fire,' answered Peter. 'I was taking a shower.' 'Come on in,' said Ed. 'Jump in the shower and wash it off. I'll find you some clothes.' When Peter closed the door behind himself in the bathroom, Ellie said 'Is it still on fire? Come on, let's go stop the fire.'

'No,' Ed said. 'I'm not going anywhere without him.'

'Why? It may be the matter of life and death. Every minute counts.'

'Whose life and death? There is nobody left inside, I hope. And why should we go there first, before he did? Isn't it his house?'

'You are . . . are . . .' Ellie was looking for the right word. At this moment, Peter appeared at the bathroom door, dressed in a bright Hawaiian shirt and shorts Ed found him.

'I've told you, I'm good at choosing clothes,' Ed said to Ellie. 'Doesn't it suit him?'

The three of them rushed to Peter's place now and stopped the fire. 'How did it start?' Ed asked when everything was over. 'I don't know,' Peter said. 'I didn't see. I was in the shower. I think somebody must have thrown something at it.'

'Why?'

'How else? I know it wasn't from the inside.'

'Maybe you did it yourself,' Ed said. 'You could do it to get an insurance, couldn't you?'

'I don't have an insurance. I mean, it's just expired,' Peter said.

'It makes it more likely that you did it yourself,' Ellie said. 'And you look like and arsonist, too.'

'Why?' Peter cried. 'I don't know how it happened, I've told you.'

'An arsonist,' Ed started, 'is somebody . . .'

'What does it matter,' Ellie asked, 'who is an arsonist?'

'Of course it does. If he is one, I'm not going to help him. I should report it, then.'

'An arsonist', Ed said again, 'is somebody who put his own or other people's possessions on fire on purpose.'

'I've told you,' Peter repeated, 'I was in the shower. I couldn't see what happened at all.'

'Why possessions?' Ellie said. 'Does it have to be somebody's possessions for the fire to matter? What if it is just a stretch of a forest?'

'If you know nothing at all about how it happened,' Ed said to Peter, 'then absolutely everything is possible. It could be you who did it. If it could be you, then you might be it, an arsonist. Then I'm not going to help you.'

'No, it can't be me. I know this much. I know it can't be me because I know I didn't do it.'

'How? And what do you mean know?'

'I know because it's me and my place.'

'You can't say 'know,' Ed interfered again. 'You don't know anything, because, as you say yourself, you haven't seen it. If you observed it properly . . .'

'What's a proper observation?'

'It's an observation you can share with other people. And also, usually, something carried out using the proper equipment.'

'What equipment? Like a camera? What's so proper about it? I hope I don't have one at my place. I'm sure I don't.'

'Ed, you have a tic about cameras,' Ellie said. 'You think about them all the time, even when a house is on fire.'

'Because they are important in this case, too. You have to agree,' Ed said to Peter, 'that if you had one, it would be possible for you to prove what actually happened. Especially, if we found at least two other people who carried out proper observations, observed the same thing and would be prepared to share what they've seen with somebody else.'

'Let's go and have another look at your place,' Ellie said.

Leaving the door of Ed and Ellie's house open, they crossed the road. The rose bushes around Peter's house looked all black and ashy. There was a big hole burned around the edges where one of the windows used to be. Otherwise everything looked fully functional, and Peter went inside. Ed and Ellie went back to their place.

'I think you are confused here,' Ellie said. 'An arsonist is not somebody who might, just might, theoretically speaking, have done it.'

'If he might, why is he not? Look, if I have, let's say, a big box, it might be used as a table. If I remove two vertical walls opposite each other, and put something on the top side, it's a table. Kind of.

From the beginning, then, it was something that might be a table. You only need to remove a wall or two of a box, to make it a table. It's the same thing with him. Remove a wall or two of his house, and it's a different thing, and he is too. He is an arsonist. And he always might be, just because walls are removable. How can you say he is not?'

'Nonsense,' Ellie said, 'and you know it yourself. Do you mean there is somebody who's reasoning just like this? Who on Earth can it be? A box is not a table. As for walls removed, I don't know . . . It's still a box for me, although maybe, just maybe, it becomes something else for the person who does it. And I think, when they are just going to do it, a box is already something not quite what it is to them. So what?'

'By the way,' Ed said, 'definitions, and this was a definition, did you get it at all? Definitions is one more thing I can do. That's why I sound a bit strange sometimes. And since I cannot sell my defining meanings' skill, I've sold the fact that I can sound strange. Do you know how?'

'How?'

'I've found an agency that helps crazy people in finding jobs. And I used it myself.'

'How?'

'There was this girl there, a real angel, Angela was her name, too, so I singled her out from the beginning. I fed her a long sad tale about depression that, I said, I've been experiencing, oh so badly, for years, and it was enough. She said it's alright. I only need somebody to confirm it. So I went to a psychiatrist I've found in the Yellow Pages and got a prescription for antidepressant drugs, once again, and when she printed it out, made her fill the form on my, what d'you call it? mental condition.'

'And?'

'And when it was done, I brought the form to Angela and signed her up as my referee. Otherwise, God only knows where I could get one. You know, I don't like these business shirts ladies much, so it's only natural that they don't like me either. But once you need a referee, you've got find one somewhere. So I found Angela and fed her a story of my depression. What's really sad about it is that I have to submit a new 'madness' confirmation form now and then, and for this, I've got, at least, to renew a drug prescription. But with cameras and the like, who will believe I'm taking it?'

'You are obsessed about cameras,' Ellie said, again. 'Next time you should get her to fill you a form for OCD. But seriously, don't you think it would be best to stay away from it all?'

'Possibly, but how? Those ladies, I mean, the ones I told you about before, you know what they think? They think something like this: you may be alright to do what you are doing, well, why not, after all, since it's a really dirty job, but tell somebody else that you're alright? Nah. This would be too much, obviously. So, you see, I needed Angela.' Ed thought for a second and added, 'Most people who sign up as mad do it for money. Or something like it, like a job. I wonder, if a job is worth it. But I seem to be the only one to ask this question.'

'Let's go for a walk,' Ellie sighed. 'We can have another look at Peter's house.' When they went out, Ellie said 'I still don't get it why you think that it's the same everywhere. Don't you think most things you told me about are just, you know, 'couleur locale?'

'Most of it is a bit like what I've seen at another place and time,' Ed said. 'But of course, I haven't seen too many places up close. Just two, in fact.'

'If you see them as alike, it's your perception, Ed,' Ellie pressed on. 'There is no real similarity.'

'Well, maybe there isn't, or maybe there is. I think, some people never fit anywhere and maybe, I am not sure, just as few fit everywhere. It just follows logically that everywhere any time is the same for them, doesn't it? Most normal people are like neither of them, are they?'

'Look, it's Peter's house,' Ellie interrupted. 'Do you think he is normal, by the way? I mean, was he today?'

Four Teas

When Ed first came to what now is his favourite café, the waiter told him that drinks there are magic, you know. They transform you into somebody new. 'What would you like?' he said.

'I'd like some tea,' Ed said. 'To warm me up'.

'We have English breakfast, Earl Grey, Vanilla Chai and Green Tea,' the waiter answered. 'Which one would you like to try today?'

Ed decided to start with—which one should he like first? English breakfast seemed like a default choice: you can hardly expect the unexpected here. Maybe Earl Grey? Or Vanilla Chai? Ed was born in Russia, in fact, but had no idea what kind of beverage would be called Vanilla Chai. Or maybe, try some Green Tea first? They say it's very energising.

After thinking it over, he decided to start with Vanilla Chai: this one was the one he was most curious about. Ed paid for tea, picked up his disposable cup and sat down to drink it at a table.

Vanilla Chai.

After a few first sips there were no more café tables and walls—he was transported in a far away place. It was a small village near Vologda. The season was winter and looking out of the window of his wooden house he could see white trees all covered with

121

snow, and, as should be, greyish smoke above the roofs. Suddenly Ed realized that he felt extremely cold and looked around himself. There must be something that would make it possible to increase the temperature inside the house. And there was, indeed, a big white clay 'pechka'—an oven—in the middle of the next room. Only it was cold. Ed wanted to start the fire, but there was no firewood inside. He got out of the house and started chopping it. One—two—three—four—he counted. Four marked a finger he nearly chopped off. It was like nothing he tried before, with any tea whatsoever, but vaguely reminded Ed how he was roaming the streets of Moscow searching for a carton of milk, also in winter. Ed finished cutting the firewood and remembered that he was a school teacher. He looked for 'valenki'—big grey felt boots—found and put them on. He started walking to the village school, getting stuck in deep white snow with every step. 'I will meet some people there', he thought. 'They might know better where to get firewood here. And if I plan to stay, I absolutely must find out when I should start planting potatoes in spring. By the way, how much do I earn?' Somehow he knew it was seven thousand roubles, but he knew just vaguely, however, what he could buy with it. He hurried on, trying to lift his feet high and avoid the deepest snow.

English breakfast tea.

'Br-r—this was cold and difficult', Ed thought when he finished his Chai tea and was transported back to his table. 'But beautiful. Where else can I see a winter like this? If only I knew things necessary to survive it. The next one I'm trying is English breakfast tea.' He bought a cup of English breakfast tea and sat down at the same table. The tea was dark and strong—the teabag was still floating in the cup. Ed decided he'd leave it there—after all, if the teabag isn't taken out, the tea gets stronger every second.

He gulped half of his cup in one swallow and found himself at a bus stop. It was ten to seven in the morning and orange Australian sun has just risen a tiny bit over the horizon line. It was very bright, and Ed felt his sunglasses in the pocket of his coat and then put them on. A few minutes later Ed got on the bus and bought himself a cheap ticket. For some mysterious reason he had no right to one, although he worked just three hours a week. These three hours were a torture to him now. Normally he worked just one hour in the morning three days a week, except for one other day—when he worked two hours in the morning, starting at the same excruciatingly early eight o'clock—unless the person he worked with decided he didn't need it. When it happened, Ed felt a certain duplicity. On the one hand, he was happy, needless to say, to sleep in. On the other hand, it meant he would lose forty dollars and, of course, like any working person, he regretted it.

Ed changed two more buses and, at three minutes past eight, as always, was there, at his destination point. His duties included showering a man in his thirties who couldn't do it for himself. At times, when Ed felt a bit more energetic and fresh, he tried to teach this man to dress. He partially succeeded, but not quite.

'Why don't they ask me to teach him how to do it?' Ed thought sometimes, when he was awake enough to think anything. 'If he could do it himself, it would save the system time and money.'

But the system didn't want to save anything—Ed knew it well—including time and money. It didn't save anything—and, perhaps, because it was so damn clumsy and undiscriminating—Ed lived off it. Not in luxury, but still . . . Unlike many other things under orange Australian sun, this turned out to be possible. Besides, he was not paid to show how to shower, he was paid to shower. And he was not qualified to show. Well, maybe he was qualified a little bit—but not all the necessary way. Not under this orange sun.

Ed finished his job, and caught a bus back. The sun was high now, and Ed put on his sunglasses and got a book out of his bag. On the way back it was always a bit more difficult to change buses, than it was when he was going there at eight o'clock. Sitting at the bus stop waiting, Ed watched people, mostly young Asians, and wondered what their English breakfast tea is like.

'Perhaps, it is better, than mine,' he decided. 'But why?'

Ed never, he suspected, got the right answer to this question. Suddenly, in the middle of his travel back from work, he was transported back to his table in the café. Ed looked inside his cup and saw there was half the tea still left in it, and the teabag was floating on the surface.

The Green Tea.

The next tea Ed wanted to try was the green one. As he ordered it and was walking towards a table, he rolled the thoughts he thought so many times in his head. People assimilate when they want to. We never change because we don't want to. It wouldn't be us if we did. It's not that we don't want to change—can you not want to do something that you cannot really imagine what it's like? What it's like when people change? Who knows? It must be a good thing, for a change, but how do you get there?

'Is it really true that we don't want to change?' Ed asked himself, partly because he couldn't think of a better question to himself. 'How big part of me is being born and raised at a certain place and time? Do I really want to give it up? How big part of me is having attended certain schools? What would be left of me, if this changed? Isn't there really something more important than this?'

'Anyway, this leads nowhere,' he decided. 'I want my green tea.' He drank it and was transformed and transported. Who he was transformed into, he couldn't quite discern at first. Was he a person repairing computers and mobile phones in one of those little shops? Or was he writing programs for the above mentioned computers? Not bad at all, but he felt it wasn't quite him. He was that person he always wanted to be who knew who to contact in China, if you want to manufacture something, literally anything, at a competitive price. And he could read and write hieroglyphs.

The green tea was not bad at all, although Ed wasn't sure where else it will take him.

Earl Grey tea.

Ed was, of course, utterly democratic in his likes and dislikes, so he was hesitant to try the last tea on the list, which was Earl Grey tea. When at last he did drink the tea, he found himself in a big suburban two-storey house. It had a seaview and when Ed looked out of the window, he could see the same orange sun, looming over the horizon, approaching sunset. The view was nice and Ed wouldn't mind enjoying it a bit longer, but the café was about to close now, and he was asked to leave. As he made his way for the exit, the waiter stopped him.

'You know,' he said, 'we have a happy hour on Friday night. You can order one tea and get one free. See what happens, if you drink two teas at once. I was told you become two different persons at the same time.'

'Wow,' Ed thought. 'The possibilities clinked and cluttered in his head, like glasses. I'll pay for one tea and get another free—and I'll be two persons at once. Or I'll get an English breakfast tea, earn some money, buy two teas and get one free. Or do I get two free then? And I'll be three or four different persons!'

The Happy Hour.

When the next week came, Ed got ready to try out combinations of different teas. He was eager to see, what he would feel like, experiencing two teas at once. 'How many different options will there be?' he asked himself and calculated. 'If you take two teas out of four at once, there are three ways to do it, if you take three out of four, you can do it in four different ways, and, of course, there is one combination of all four teas. So this makes it eight. Eight possible combinations. What do you call them? Tea cocktails, maybe? Definitely not cocktails, but what?' Eight seemed like a big number, but Ed decided he could just choose some teas to combine on a whim and see how he goes.

Vanilla Chai and English breakfast tea.

Ed picked up both teas from the counter and sat down. He was now in his home town where he went last year to see his parents. He was himself, Ed English breakfast. Snaps of his last year experience flashed in his memory and he half-closed his eyes to see them better. The best thing about going home was there was something he could do there that he couldn't do where he drank his English breakfast tea, and earn some money in an acceptable way. He also felt like he had lived and was still living two lives and, somehow, he felt it was his advantage. Why? He couldn't tell. He wondered what it would be like, if he wouldn't have stayed in that place where he had come years ago, when he first left home for a faraway land. What if he moved somewhere else after this, and then, again, somewhere else? Would he be feeling now that he has had three or more different lives? Or was two the limit?

His school friends had jobs and careers and earned significantly more, than Ed could think of, when he visited his home town, although this was noticeably better, than what Ed could count on where he drank his English breakfast. He felt like he got stuck forever in that part of his life that he once left home, when he departed for the English breakfast land. And stuck at that point in time, now many years ago, when he's done it. He was still a twenty something in everything that had something to do with home. He spoke the language that was spoken then, and his tastes were those that were in fashion back then. People who he shared these tastes with couldn't now retrieve them from memory.

He couldn't understand how these people's children could have grown up so fast and they themselves could have changed so much. He himself got older and wiser, of course, and cherished this fact a lot, since it was about the only thing he could show off for all this time that had gone. He felt wonderful, in a way: there were more than one of him and these two were completely different persons living in different historical and geological formations. The only thing he was not sure about is that anybody else could understand how many of him there were and which one there were talking to at the moment.

English breakfast mixed with Earl Grey.

Ed poured a bit of each tea in an empty glass and sipped. He just came after a rather long and tiring trip to his client's home. Somehow something always happened when he had to do it, especially for the first time. Today was Sunday and he had to go by railway on the other end of the city. It proved to be not that easy. The trains have been cancelled and he had to catch a replacement bus. He would have been late, which can be quite unfortunate in this situation, if it wasn't for the fact that he had an extra half an hour to get there. 'Why did it happen?' Ed wondered. 'Why does it happen, apparently, too often? It could be a coincidence, of course. Who knows?' Thinking about what we can rightly call a coincidence, Ed knocked on the door. He was not, despite everything, even a minute late. Suddenly, as he heard somebody's steps on the other side of the door, 'I don't want to come here and test the limits of coincidence each week,' he said to himself.

Somebody let him in and he met Meryl, his new client. She was a young good looking woman who was suddenly left quadriplegic by a sudden bout of a mysterious disease. She was lying in a room next to the entrance door, between an electric hoist and a rather old-fashioned dressing table with lots of dolls and cosmetic bottles on it. Ed looked up and could see that a wall cracked inside the room and a black zigzag starting in the corner of the ceiling was spreading down, obviously threatening to break the room off altogether. The sight was depressing and the trip here so long and full of unexpected!

The first thing Meryl wanted him to do was to make some tea for her and himself. Ed went to the kitchen and poured some hot water into two cups with Earl Grey tea bags. He took the cups back to the room and started manipulations necessary for the morning shower of his client. Ed bent her leg in the knee and turned her on her side, put her sling under and rolled her back. As he leaned over the woman, his feet unexpectedly slipped and went up in the air, and his head, now very small ('why is it so small,' Ed thought feverishly 'did I try this tea in the kitchen? What kind of tea is it?') dove into the cup. A moment later he was swimming in the cup of hot tea, splashing the water with his legs and arms.

'God, this is hot,' Ed thought. 'But it smells nice, like nothing else. If this was milk, and I was a frog,' he thought a minute later, 'I should have tried to work hard enough to beat it into butter and then get out of the cup. I wonder if one can beat Earl Grey tea into butter?'

As Ed was trying to solve this pressing question, he swam in circles around the edge of the cup. After a while, the tea cooled a bit, and its level lowered, as Ed was splashing a lot of water out of the cup in his efforts. Ed found a deep scratch on the inside of the cup, placed his foot firmly in the step, pulled himself up and got out of the cup. He was soaked. His client was still hanging in the air where he left her before he fell in the cup.

'Should I ask her for a change of clothes,' Ed thought. 'Or put her down first and wheel into the shower?'

It's too painful to describe what he did first and how. Let's just say that he did get out of the door on that day and caught a scheduled train back.

English breakfast mixed with green tea and Earl Grey.
Every now and then Ed attended meetings for people who did the same kind of work as he did. They were lively and interesting and he liked them. At one such meeting they were instructed by a supervising person, conducting the meeting, to engage in a role play. In a group of three, one person had to impersonate a client needing support, and the other two—his potential support workers (which is what they were called). The task of the interview was to find out each other's preferences of time, place, the length and

nature of work, and other important things. The other two people in Ed's group were a middle-aged Chinese woman who did more work hours, than any of the other fifteen people in the room, and a young girl, who once escaped some kind of illness which nearly left her quadriplegic, but didn't. 'Hers was, in fact, quite a fairy tale story,' Ed thought sometimes with a feeling which would be difficult to define. The role play interview went like this.

'When do you want to start in the morning?' Ed asked the girl who represented the client.

'Eight o'clock,' she answered.

'This is early,' the Chinese woman sang. 'Why?'

'Really, why eight o'clock?' he asked, too.

'I have to get ready for my classes,' the girl said. 'I go to study and must be there at nine. I want to have a breakfast, before I go. Coffee and a croissant is fine.'

'What nationality are you?' the Chinese woman asked, suddenly. It wasn't quite out of place, however, because nationality was one of the questions on the list that they had to cover.

'France,' said the girl. She spoke without an accent. 'My nationality is France.'

'No,' said the Chinese woman. 'Fren-ch is a nationality. France is a place. Why France?'

'I was born there,' said the girl. 'But I'm not French, you see. My nationality is France.'

For some reason, Ed remembered this mock conversation long after it was finished. But of course, it was just a role play, with no names and reliable indications of places.

How Magic, Tajik and Logic got together with Mata Hari

A very short and absurd play.

ACT 1.

Magic is walking along the road, looking sad. Tajik is walking along the same road towards her. When they meet, they start talking.

Tajik.	Hullo, what's your name?
Magic.	Ma-geek.
Tajik.	Ma-geek? Lovely name. What does it mean?
Magic.	It means I'm a geek. Because it's me, it's called ma-geek.
Tajik.	What is it used for?
Magic.	For freaks. Have you heard of geeks and freaks?
Tajik.	No. But I believe you. Actually, I suspect you mispronounce it. It's magic, madgic, not ma-geek. Nice to meet you Magic. My name is Tajik.
Magic.	Hi.
Tajik.	You see, our names sound similar. I'm a Tajik, and you are Ma-gic.

Magic.   I'm not a mujik, I'm Magic.

Tajik.   Yeah-yeah. I mean your jik is called magic and my gic is called Tajik. Why? It's my jik, so what sense does it make to call it tajik?

Magic.   What is this gic thing anyway?

Tajik.   This is what we are trying to find. Once we'll get a jik somewhere, we'll have a good look at it. But listen, I've got another idea. If we put ma and ta together, we won't be confused which one is which, and who does it belong to. Mata Jik. Sounds nice, doesn't it?

Magic.   I've never heard of Mata Jik. But there is Mata Hari. Here she is.

Mata Hari (very beautiful and smiling). Hullo, how are you?

Magic and Tajik, together. Good, yourself?

Mata Hari. Good, thank you. I've come to tell you an important information. There is a spy amongst you.

Magic and Tajik, together. A spy, really? Awful. What's her name?

Mata Hari. Her name is Logic. Look here—see—she is perched on a tree over there. You must knock her down, guys, she is dangerous like this.

Magic and Tajik, together. Yeah, but how? How can we knock her down?

Mata Hari. You can throw something at her.

Tajik.   We can put a few things on each other and reach the top branch where she is. Or, maybe, build something next to the tree—a house, or a temple. Then from the top of it we can reach the tree.

Magic.   No, no. Let's just shake the tree. If we shake hard enough, she is going to fall.

Mata Hari. (mumbling to herself). Did she really say this?

Magic comes close to the tree and starts shaking. Leaves and little twigs are falling off, but Logic is clinging to the branch, clutching it with her hands. Magic shakes harder. Logic lets go of the tree and falls down.

Logic.　　　Ouch. It hurts. Why are you doing this?

Magic, Tajik and Mata Hari, together. You are a spy.

Logic.　　　No. I'm not a spy. Please, don't shake me anymore. It hurts.

Magic.　　　Can you prove you are not a spy?

Logic.　　　Prove it? Yes. Yes, of course. What do spies do? I suppose, they spy. I spy with my little eye something beginning with an I.

Mata Hari.　See, you spy. You say so yourself.

Logic.　　　　It's not this kind of spying. It's spying in a different sense. It's not spying at all.

Magic and Tajik, together. Keep these sophisms for yourself. A spy is a spy. Spying is spying. You are spying. You said so yourself.

Logic.　　　No. I was just quoting what people say when they play a game. Trying to remember what I know about spying. Look, this is all I know. I've got no idea what spies do. Please let me go.

Mata Hari.　Do you promise not to spy?

Majik and Tajik, together. She's got an eye, how can she not to spy?

Magic.　　　Really, if you saw something, it can be as dangerous as a saw.

Tajik.　　　Not 'you saw', 'you've seen'. It's present perfect. Well, it's present perfect in most cases, but I'm not sure when precisely. Sometimes it can be 'you saw'. But it's not dangerous at all.

Mata Hari.　So, what's the solution?

Logic.　　　What solution? Please, don't make it too strong.

Magic.　　　Have mercy on her. Look, maybe we can use her in a positive way. We can use her when we all go looking for jik.

ACT 2.

Logic.   I'm not really a spy you see. I know who is a real spy. It's Red Herring.

Magic and Tajik. Red Herring, why?

Mata Hari. Why Red Herring?

Logic.   Firstly, it's red. Isn't it enough reason?

Mata Hari.   No, be reasonable. Red herrings have something to do with the state system. They cannot be spies by definition.

Logic.   Why? I can't see it. Everybody else can, and they can't. Aren't they a kind of privileged part of our er . . . society? Well, I guess it shows they aren't, because they can't.

Magic.   Can't what?

Logic.   Can't be spies.

Majik and Tajik. You know very little. Red herrings don't have to be statutory . . . no, what is it? Statistic . . . stately . . . Maybe, statuesque? Whatever it is, they don't have to be any of this. Avoid stereotyping, for God's sake. Red Herrings can originate on an individual level. In this case, maybe, they can be spies?

Mata Hari. I really feel I won't know what they are before I see it. I've never encountered a single one, believe it or not.

Logic.   I know where we can find one. See that big black wall over there. Come closer and you'll see one hanging on a hook.

Magic and Tajik. A red herring, hanging on a hook? How can it be? Let's see for ourselves.

    Magic, Tajik, Logic and Mata Hari come closer and see a red herring hanging on a hook. They start talking to him.

Magic and Tajik. Who are you?

133

Red Herring.   I'm a red herring, can't you see it?

Mata Hari. Why on Earth are you red?

Red Herring.   They painted me red.

Logic.   Who are they?

Red Herring.   Those people who hung me here.

Magic and Tajik. Why did they do it? Why did they paint you red? Why did they hang you?

Red Herring. They painted me red because they wanted. If something is yours, you can paint it any colour you want. They hung me by the neck for a crime, of course.

Magic and Tajik. This is terrible, what crime was it?

Red Herring. It was a crime of passion. I was a pirate, on a pirate ship.

Logic.   Where was it? Was it White or Barents Sea? Herring, of course is a very foreign sounding word. Some people even think that all herring in a jar is simply not done. I mean, not ready to eat.

Red Herring. That's why they hung me by the neck on the wall and painted red. To make me ready to eat and more digestible. But I must tell you, you are wrong about herring being a foreign sounding word. It can be called rolled mops, you know, and it's nearly the same product.

Logic.   Herring, you are a fish, aren't you? How can you be hung by the neck? Do fish have necks?

Mata Hari. Generally they don't, but if you need to hang one, they may as well do.

Logic.   Is not having a neck counted as a disability, I wonder? Even if you are a fish?

Tajik.   Nah, not if you are a fish.

Mata Hari. This can be confusing. There are some damn strange fishes out there. What about swordfish? Doesn't it have a neck?

Logic.   You can say it does, but it grows on the other side of the head.

Mata Hari. So you see, fishes can have necks, even if they grow in all the wrong directions. It means, by the way, that if a fish doesn't have one, it's a disability.

Tajik.   All because of that damn swordfish?

Magic.   Why not? Do you mind it, if fishes will be obliged to have necks?

Logic.   What about sawfish? Does it have a neck, if we need to hang one?

Mata Hari. Oh please, forget about necks, just for now. What crime did they hang you for, Red Herring? Were you really a spy?

Red Herring. No, of course, I wasn't. I hate all kinds of paperwork, as it's totally against my inclinations and temperament. I was a pirate on a pirate ship, out there with my mates.

Logic.   A noticeboard next to your head says you were a spy.

Red Herring. I can't reach it, because I'm hung by the neck. But maybe you can correct the mistake?

Mata Hari. It's engraved in the metal.

Logic.   It was nice to have met you. We must go now. Who would believe that red herrings are such nice guys?

Magic, Tajik, Logic and Mata Hari say good bye to Red Herring and go away. Red Herring is left on the wall, hung by the neck.

ACT 3.

Logic.   I think now it's time to find out what that jik thing is. What do you think it could be?

Tajik.   It's something magical—because it's in magic—and it's also very clever—because it's in logic.

Mata Hari. It's something like a philosopher's stone.

Magic.   What's a philosopher's stone? Or is it the philosopher's stone? Is there one or many?

Mata Hari. Originally there was one, but, of course, you can break it into many. It all depends on the pressure you apply. In the Middle Ages, they believed, wrongly, of course, that it turns all kinds of matter into gold.

Tajik.   What does it look like? And where can it be found?

Mata Hari. What do you think it looks like? What turns all kinds of matter into gold?

Logic.   If somebody asked me, I would say it's conformism.

Magic, Tajik and Mata Hari together. What? What the hell is this? What does it look like?

Logic.   I am not sure what it looks like, because I had a chance to see one only from a distance. As far as I could figure out, it's a kind of stone. A semi-precious stone, beautiful, but non-transparent. Something like opal. It can appear to be any colour, depending on what side of it you turn up. It works like this. When you throw it at something, or better somebody, it turns it into dust or changes its shape. This is why it is called con-form-ism. The stone itself returns to the thrower full of gold.

Magic.   What do you mean returns to the thrower? Does it go along the same line it has been thrown?

Logic.   No, not quite like this. It's not a boomerang, mind you.

Mata Hari. We need to organize an expedition and test some of these philosopher's stones of yours in action. What do you mean, they return back full of gold? What are they, golden nuggets?

Logic.   I don't know. Some may be nuggets with golden ore and some are just bottles or other containers which become filled with golden dust once you throw them.

Magic and Tajik. We'll see.

In the next scene Magic, Tajik, Logic and Mata Hari find themselves in a pleasant street of a small Australian town.

Magic and Tajik. We can try it here. It's pretty quiet.

Tajik.   We can't throw stones at people as an experiment. Let's find some animals or other inferior creatures to try it on.

Logic.   What animals?

Mata Hari. Any will do. Kangaroos. Or, maybe, possums. Or best of all, cats and dogs, because they are not protected by law and are threatening Australian wildlife themselves.

Logic.   I can see a magpie over there on a tree.

Magic and Tajik. They can be quite aggressive, especially in spring. Let's try it. Will any stone do?

Mata Hari. Yes, if you throw it in the right way.

Logic picks up a stone from the ground, aims carefully and throws it at the magpie. The magpie takes off and moves to another tree. The stone falls down on the ground. A minute later Magic, Tajik, Logic and Mata Hari can see the magpie to pick up the stone from the ground and fly away.

Magic.   Let's not throw anything at magpies anymore. They've got such big beaks. And it's really difficult not to miss them, especially when they are out there in a tree.

Logic.   Let's start with somebody who'd be an easier target.

Tajik.   Maybe a koala? They sleep all day. Won't even see somebody is going to throw a stone at them. And it's probably them or somebody like them who this technique was developed for.

Mata Hari. Good idea.

Magic.   I can see a koala over there on top of a eucalyptus.

Tajik.   They are so harmless and sleepy. I'm not sure I want to. Besides, they are protected by law.

Mata Hari. We'll try, just once. Look, she is in a really good position up there on a branch, directly above us. If we throw a stone at her, it will fall down to us. It's the law of gravitation.

Logic. OK. Let's just do it.

Logic picks up a stone and throws it. The stone doesn't quite reach the koala in a tree, but when it falls down, they all move their heads together to have a close look at it, and can see that the stone has turned pure gold.

Magic. Look, it's turned golden, but the koala is where she was, safe and sound. How can this be?

Mata Hari to Tajik. It's because you've had so much moral scruples about throwing it at this koala. Of course, Logic couldn't help but miss her. The stone has turned golden anyway, to reward you.

Logic. I want to try it at somebody who I wouldn't want to miss.

Mata Hari. Do you have any enemies? Who is it?

Logic. No. Of course, not. (after a short pause). Oh! I know who would be a good socially acceptable target for throwing stones.

Magic, Tajik and Mata Hari together. Who?

Logic. Molvanian terrorists.

Magic and Mata Hari. Excellent idea!

Tajik. Molvanian terrorists? Sounds vaguely familiar, but who are they? Where is Molvania?

Logic. Molvania is somewhere in Eastern Europe. It might be one of those states which are on the map one day and tomorrow they mightn't be. It's not necessarily funny for those involved, but for some people it is.

ACT 4.

A tank full of Molvanian terrorists is moving up the street. Magic, Tajik, Mata Hari and Logic are watching it from a pedestrian path.

Logic.   Let's try another kind of philosopher's stones at them.
Magic.   What kind?
Logic.   I have a few philosopher's stones here—let's call them phi stones, shall we? They look like bottles—or other plastic containers. When you throw one at somebody, if you aim really well and don't miss them, this person becomes a liquid in a container. They just evaporate and then condense into a liquid inside the bottle.
Mata Hari.   What can you do with the liquid? Can you pour it inside some other container?
Logic.   Sure, anything. Or you can put it in the fridge and once it gets settled, I beg your pardon, set, tip the ice out on a plate.
Tajik.   Here comes a Molvanian tank. Let's try it. One, two, three—throw.

Logic throws a plastic box at one of the people in the tank. At this moment, a big brave-looking man touched by the container disappears. The container lands on the roof of the moving tank and fills up with a brownish green liquid.

Mata Hari.   Look, we got one, but the other two are still sitting there, safe and sound. It looks like we need enough containers to liquidize them all, one for each person.
Tajik.   Can we pour a couple of different persons in the same bottle, for economy sake? To save space?
Mata Hari.   No, this is impossible.

Magic.   Let's try another, friendlier approach. Maybe, we can
              seduce some of them?
Tajik.   Molvanian terrorists, you know, as far as I can imagine,
              are not necessarily love hungry throughout their life.
              Maybe they satisfied their love hunger in Molvania, if
              they ever had one, in the first place?
Magic.   Let's try, let's try. It's a question of honour. What do you
              think can attract them?
Tajik.   I don't know. What would you think?
Magic.   I don't know either, but if I was in their place, I would
              love to be poured into some attractive container.
Mata Hari.   An attractive container like what?
Magic.   An attractive container which has something to do with
              what they want.
Logic.   What do you think they want? Money? Fame? Love?
Mata Hari.   Let's fill a bottle with some gold sand at the bottom and
              then fill the rest of it up with a Molvanian terrorist or
              two, in a few layers. It's called sand art.

    Logic fills a plastic bottle with some gold sand and throws it at
the people in the tank.

Logic.   Once one of them liquidizes in the bottle, it means
              they are married to a good member of the mainstream
              society.

    The plastic bottle half-filled with gold sand touches one of the
people in the tank, but nothing happens.

Magic.   Oy, all the sand got spilled out in the air.
Logic.   We need a cork or a lid.
Mata Hari.   How are they going to get inside, then?
Tajik.   No, this is not going to work. It doesn't look like they
              want to be seduced, at least, not by us.

Logic.   There must be another way to contain them all in containers of the necessary shape.

Mata Hari.   If we can't seduce them, maybe, we can induce them to do something.

Logic.   Do something like what?

Mata Hari.   Like say something reasonable.

Logic.   I know what to do. We'll throw a phi-stone container at them, and it'll take the shape of a speech bubble with words we want to hear. After all, all containers are made of bubbles. Or they used to be. One, two, three!

Logic throws a phi-stone at one of the Molvanian terrorists. A speech bubble, which is exactly the same shape as the phi-stone, appears at his mouth.

Molvanian terrorist. I would do anything to belong with you, kill and steal included.

Logic.   Please don't, this wouldn't be good. There are other ways to be included. Promise you won't.

CURTAIN.

Logic.   Lift the curtain, I've just remembered what jik means.

Magic.   What?

Nature and Nurture

Man.
Woman.
Three bulls.
A cow.
Heim the bullfighter.
Vania Juanito.

Prologue.

Woman.	(opens an oven). Good Heavens, I've nearly burned it again! Why does it always happen? What were you thinking, by the way? Are you going to eat it, or not?
Man.	Burned what? I didn't even know, there was something in there.
Woman.	The cake, the cake.
Man.	Oh, the cake. Another cake again . . . You are a terrible cook, it's just your nature, admit it.
Woman.	Not at all. It's not my nature and not my fault.
Man.	On the contrary, if it was your nature, it wouldn't be your fault. We can't control the nature. If it's not your nature, it must be your fault.

Woman. Why must? If not the nature? I mean, you are going to eat it, as well as I do, if it turns out good, but whatever happens to it, is my fault, not yours. Do you think it's fair? Anyway, nobody has ever shown to me, how to make this kind of pudding.

Man. Pudding? Somehow it rings strange for what you are doing. Anyway, if you can't do it, because they've never shown to you how, it's your nurture, not nature, that has to be blamed. It's an old problem, called 'nature and nurture'. Why cannot there be a Jewish bullfighter? Or a female one? What would happen, if you take a rabbi's son and raise him as a torero? Do you think he'll put up a good corrida?

Woman. Yeah, why not. People are made by their upbringing. But the strange thing is, some of these crazy combinations happen to happen in real life and some don't.

Man. What crazy combinations?

Woman. I've seen a Chinese bullfighter once.

Man. Really? Where?

Woman. No, just kidding. Almost. I've seen a Chinese man talk about corrida. But it didn't sound at all, like he could be fulfilling bullfighter's functions. He was all reserve and measurement and concentrated mostly on what was the angle of that sharp thing, whatever it is, the spear or something, to the bull's body.

Man. So, what's the angle?

Woman. I don't know, he gave us some numbers, but I've forgotten. Anyway, the angle is forever changing, as the bull is jumping and running, until he is dead. It's a bit like nature and nurture.

Man. Why? It's too poetic. And anyway, nature is a permanent, constant thing, unlike anything else.

Woman. Why poetic? What's so poetic about bullfighting? Or maybe there is something, I don't know, I suppose you've got to try it, to tell. And you are wrong about nature, too. It is not constant. One minute later you are not the same, as a minute before it.

Man.	It's because of nurture.
Woman.	How do you know?
Man.	Think about it this way. Nature is like a rock and nurture is like a wave. Or a sea tide.
Woman.	But every single wave that breaks against the rock is different. And eventually the rock gets eroded, too. You can never tell what's what.
Man.	What do you mean what's what? What's what in what?
Woman.	I mean, the whole point of differentiating . . . It's such a long word, sorry. I can't do without it. I wonder, do all long words we use, come from nurture? Because, obviously, words like differentiating cannot be in our nature, can they? Not mine, anyway. I mean the whole point of differentiating between nature and nurture is that you can tell, theoretically speaking, at least, what's caused by nature and what's, on the other hand, by nurture.
Man.	How do you tell?
Woman.	Take identical twins,. separated at birth. Their nature is exactly the same, but, once they are separated, the nurture is different. So you can tell, what's what.
Man.	Do you have to have twins? Wouldn't just a pair of siblings do? I used to know a boy, who was a son of a Spanish man, who was raised in a Russian village after the war. I wonder, if he had an identical twin somewhere. That would be handy.
Woman.	You mean the boy or his father?
Man.	Doesn't matter.
Woman.	Yes, it does. What are they, like clones of each other? Each next one of an exactly same nature as the previous one. Your first Spaniard's nature must have

been changed after he'd lived in a Russian village for so many years.

Man.   Yeah, maybe. I don't know what it was like, before he came, in the first place.

Woman.   It's a bit like a big matrioshka. Whatever is the biggest outward shell—call it nature or nurture, you can open it up and find another thing inside, and then open it up and find another. Nurture inside nature, and then inside it nurture again.

Man.   I wonder if somebody could make a bullfighter out of you. Or what happens, if we take a bullfighter and dress him in a matrioshka's dress.

Woman.   It should work all right. There is so much red in it.

ACT 1.

There are three big bulls on the stage. Next to them one can see a crate full of red silk strips. Heim is walking nervously up and down, staring at the bulls, as he passes by. He is getting ready for a corrida.

Man.   What's going on? When are we going to start?

Woman.   Yes, when? I can't wait.

Heim.   They'll give a signal. You'll hear them shoot.

Man.   Why are there three bulls?

Heim.   I can try them all, whichever is best. Or, maybe, I'll do all three at once, to save the time. I'm feeling brave today.

Woman.   What about the cow? What is she here for?

Heim.   I'm not sure, but I think she is a replacement. Once I've finished with the bulls, I can do her.

Woman.   Excellent. Do you know how to wave the red cloth?

Heim.   I've never tried, but I think I can. It will come naturally to me.

Supervisor.   Just before we start, I want to give you some advice. It's up to you, how many bulls you choose to have on stage with you, at once. You can have all three or just one, or maybe two. Whatever you find works best for you. By the way, these bulls aren't just any simple ones. They understand the human language. You can try talking to them, while fighting, and maybe you'll find it helps you in the process.

A minute after Heim, Man, Woman, thee bulls and a cow hear a signal to start. Everyone lifts their head up, to see where it comes from. Heim runs onto the stage with a square piece of red silk and starts lunging before one of the bulls.

Woman.   What are you doing?
Heim.   Can't you see? Teasing him. Trying to make him angry.

Heim lunges once more, waving a piece of red before the bull. The bull steps back, to be out of his way.

Man.   He is not aggressive. No good for the game. You'll have to try another.
Heim.   I just haven't found the right approach yet. Maybe, he doesn't care about this strip of red silk, but there must be something else that works. Everybody is aggressive, if you find the right approach. I mean, you just gotta know, what works as a red cloth.
Woman.   (shouts from her seat). What kind of bull are you? You are a real cow, indeed.
Cow.   Very tru-ue. I'm not afraid of you-ou at all.

The bull starts looking more involved, as he hears that. He makes one step forward, and as Heim runs away with his red cloth, along the edge of the arena, starts chasing him. They will make a couple of circles, when Heim notices that the other two bulls are running, too.

Heim.	(to Woman). You were talking to one of them, this big one, but it worked for all of them. They are all angry now. I can even see the froth on their mouth.
Man.	What do you mean by 'their mouth'? They've got three.
Heim.	Yes, I know. But it looks like one. They are all frothed.
Woman.	Why is their reaction so much alike? They run together and froth together.
Heim.	Birds of a feather, you know, they flock . . .
Woman.	Together. Why?
Heim.	It's the instinct. It's got something to do with safety and procreation. They feel safe, when they flock, and it's easier to find a mate for procreation.
Woman.	But it's disgusting. They do everything together, even get angry. One bull's mouth is wet with froth and all the other follow . . . One starts running . . .
Heim.	And the other bulls follow. They start stampeding—get out of the way or you'll get squashed. It's nature. None of the things which are natural is disgusting—or so I've been taught.
Man.	None? None whatsoever? I wonder, if one can make them behave differently, though. You know, make one bull run, and the other two stand still. Try.
Heim.	Let's think logically. If one of them was blind, and wouldn't see a red silk strip, maybe I could. But as it is . . . I'm not sure. Blindness is a great individuator. Is there such a word? If I wanted to sound pathetic, I'd say that if you don't see, where everybody is running, maybe you see something else. You know, with your inner vision. But naturally, it's safer to see, where everybody is running. There is no doubt about it.
Heim.	Listen, I've come up with a joke, to cheer you up.
Woman.	Yes?
Heim.	What's in common between a pack of dogs and a talk show? The way participants communicate. One

starts barking and the other join in, barking the same thing.

Man.   Not all talk shows are like this. You see a lot of independent thought expressed in some of them.

Heim.   Yes, no doubt about it. The question is, you know, whether it's punishable and in what way. But what's the difference between the two?

Woman.   Yes, what's the difference?

Heim.   You know, what binds together the participants of an average talk show: it's their social survival instinct. But it's not all that clear about dogs. Who knows what is it that keeps them together?

Man.   This is sad, man. Do you really think we haven't gone that far from animals?

Heim.   It depends on how you look at it. Why, do you think, all chimps in a group attack an intruder together? What would happen to the chimp who'd try to befriend him?

Man.   At the very least, he'd be a permanent omega in his herd. Or maybe, the other would kill him altogether.

Heim.   Exactly. But why?

Man.   I don't know. Why? I think, it's somehow in their nature, that they all follow the leader, an alpha male chimp, and do the same thing.

Heim.   Yes, exactly. And we are just the same, only we are supposed to think and articulate. But listen, why does the alpha male hate the intruder so much?

Man   I don't know. Why? I guess I'm no alpha male, or I'd give you an answer.

Heim.   The alpha is afraid for his place in the hierarchy, because he doesn't know, what to expect from an intruder. So he attacks him, to prevent his downfall. The other just follow him, although it might be completely irrational for them. It's their nature to obey an alpha.

Man.   It makes some sense. I wonder, however, whether this picture is accurate. Can you, somehow, breed or nurture disobedience in them at all?

Heim.   You mean, teach monkeys to disobey? Or teach it to the bulls? Or do you suppose they are all the same?

Woman. Yeah. Make a dissident out of a bull. And play corrida with him. Do you think it's possible?

Man.   I'd try it with this deaf one. But who said he is deaf at all? Maybe, he is just foreign?

Heim.   This is freaky. I am going to freak out, if we proceed like this. Let's try something different. Do you think, they'd understand jokes?

Woman. Who? Bulls?

Man.   I don't think so, but does it matter much? Many people don't, either. Although they think, they do, when bulls, you can claim, haven't even heard of humour. Would you say, it makes them superior or inferior to seriously minded humans, if both don't understand it, anyway? I mean, humans could have, because they are, at least, aware, that there is humour. You know, if you know, that there's something to understand here, maybe you'd get it then, but, if you know it and don't get it, it's obviously hopeless.

Heim.   Yes. I suppose, you are right. One thing I know and don't quite get is, why are seriously-minded so serious? By the way, is serious the same root as serial? And why does serial sound like cereal? And surreal? Because you see, if all these things are related, it starts making some sense.

Woman. How does it make sense?

Heim.   Just a moment, I will explain. Remember, at school they told us, that people of Ancient Rome were always hungry for bread and circus, or food and entertainment.

Maybe, some wanted more bread, which has become morning cereal these days, and other wanted more circus. Those who wanted cereal more, than circus, have become serially serious. Can it be true?

Man.   You skip the most important thing. Why was it? Why did some Romans plant cereals, when other watched circus? Was it a natural innate difference, or a product of their environment?

Heim.   Of course, it was the work of their environment. Slaves planted cereals, and the patrician elite watched the gladiators' fights. Most of them were born to whatever position they were in, so it was innate, you can claim.

Woman.   Are you saying understanding humour is innate? Or, do you think, it's something we learn as children?

Man.   Great question. Can't it be both, I always wonder?

Woman.   Who do you mean both? Have you got another woman?

Man.   You are not following. I mean . . .

Woman.   (interrupting). Of course, I'm not following you. I've got some dignity. If anything, you have a mobile.

Heim.   Cool down, guys. Let's teach these bulls a couple of jokes. It will shed some light on that innate question.

Man.   Bulls? Teach a couple of jokes? How?

Heim.   We'll start with some simple ones. Just to give them an idea of what laughter is like.

Woman.   Simple jokes like what?

Heim.   We can try and tickle them. Are they going to laugh?

Woman.   Tickle? You go ahead, I won't. Anyway, it's funnier, if you do it.

Heim.   Why? What, if it's just the opposite? Try, you may even find it pleasant.

Woman.   Pleasant? Nah . . . I don't think so. I'm a very hedonistic person, you see. But there is nothing hedonistic about tickling these particular bulls. I don't foresee any pleasure. Unless, of course, it's an emotional turmoil you are after. It's a kind of masochistic pleasure.

Heim.   I just assumed . . .

Woman.   You assumed wrongly. I wouldn't tickle any of these bulls, if somebody paid me. Unless, of course, it would be a hugely big sum. Then maybe I would imagine that some of these bulls are Robert de Niro, and tickle. Who else can come up with a hugely big sum? Would you say he looks like a bull? Do you think he'd understand humour? (to Heim). You try tickling yourself.

Heim tickles one of the bulls.

Heim.   He is not laughing. (to Man). Now you try it, just in case you've got a lighter touch.

Man tickles another bull and it starts giggling.

Man.   Look, look here you both. It worked! I wonder, if it's because I've tried another bull, or is it because I'm the best person at tickling among all of you?

Heim.   Yes. Is it nature—the bull is different—or nurture—he is being tickled by another person? Anyway, he is laughing, can you believe it?

Man.   But look, between the two of us, it's also the question of nature and nurture. Am I better at tickling, because I'm just naturally better, or did somebody show me how to do it? I know nobody's ever shown it to me, so it's just my nature. Somehow it always feels better, to be naturally better.

Woman.   I think it's nice to know you've learned it and so deserve all the praise. A friend of mine . . . No, my grandfather's friend used to say: women like to learn, but men are born with a natural knowledge of nature. They know how and why the wheel is spinning, but women need to look at it and think first. But some things can never be taught to men, however hard you try.

Man.   Things like what?

Woman.   Never mind, I don't want to explain. It's just my intuition.

Heim.   This is getting sad and personal. What's the next joke we are going to show them? Or should we, I mean you, Man, tickle the other bulls first, for a full comparison?

Man.   I think it's enough. We now know that they can be, in principle, tickled to giggle. Nobody knows, anyway, what it depends on, whether they actually do. But when one does start laughing, the other two will join in, without being tickled.

Woman.   Precisely. Maybe some of them don't giggle, just because they don't want that bell on their neck to ring.

Man.   That would be nurture. Bells are not part of our nature, are they?

Heim.   But whether they like the sound of it, may well be. When they giggle, the bells jingle. Some like it, some don't.

Woman.   I know, what other joke we can teach them.

Man and Heim, together. What? Do you have an idea?

Woman.   Yes. Or, maybe, I should rather say it's been shown to me many times. You know, in slapstick, when somebody stumbles and falls down, it's always supposed to be funny? It's so simple, that I think we can try it on them.

Heim.   Bulls don't stumble. Maybe, it's because they have four legs, instead of two.

Man.   If more legs means better balance, the most well-balanced creature on Earth must be a centipede. Sounds plausible. I know, what we can do. Each of them has only one tail.

	We can pull them by this tail and then let go. See what will happen?
Woman.	They will run forward a bit, trying to free themselves, and then fall down on all four.
Man.	Yes. And if we do this to only one of them, the other two may find it funny. Let's try it now.

Heim comes close to one of the bulls and starts pulling its tail. The animal freezes for a moment, as if astonished, and starts pulling forward with all its might. Heim keeps him at his tail length for a few seconds, and then lets go. As expected, the bull crashes down into the big yellow wall before him and falls down. The other two bulls start giggling.

Woman.	See? It worked. It always does. Now we know, that both of them can giggle.
Heim.	Why do you think they find it funny?
Woman.	Everybody does. I think, it's the innate competitiveness streak inside any living creature, that makes it funny. You take a tail or make up one, if it's not long enough as it is, and pull it. The result is always funny.
Man.	You are somewhat confused here. You pull someone's leg, not a tail. I guess it's got something to do with what's called a healthy aggression.
Woman.	Yes, healthy it is. How do you know which aggression is healthy? Do you think we should pull their legs as well and see, what's going to happen?

ACT 2.

The same arena with three bulls and a cow, standing near the edge.

Heim (to Woman). It's your turn now. You'll be a bullfighter.
Woman.   Me? What makes you think I can do it?

Man.	Of course you can. Just try some kind of new approach. That's how new approaches are made. If you cannot pull through what other people can.
Woman.	To pull what through what? Do you mean a leg or a tale? I suppose to pull a tale through, it has to be truthful. If a tale is true, you can pull it through the hearer's ears. Otherwise . . . What happens otherwise?
Heim.	Otherwise it gets stuck in one ear like a piece of wax.
Woman.	Hot?
Heim.	I don't know. Earwax is never hot, is it? Or do you mean the tale?
Woman.	I'm totally confused now. Do I need some kind of tale, true or not, to play with these bulls? Why? I think I'll just ride one of them.
Heim.	Try it. But you'll see you need a tale, preferably a new one.
Woman.	A new tale? I can never make a new tale. Women are conservationists, not creationists by nature.
Man.	You mean you are conservative, rather than creative. Not a conservationist, rather than creationist.
Woman.	What's the difference?
Heim.	It's a world of difference. Creationists believe in God who created the world. Conservationists are people who think we spoil this world too much too fast, and try to do something about it. To be creative.
Woman.	To do something like what?
Heim.	Like create a new kind of fuel. Conservative people, on the other hand, want everything to be the same.
Woman.	But what's women's role in it?
Man.	In the end of the day, it's because of them there are so many people.
Woman.	Do you think it shows they are conservative or creative?
Man.	I don't know. What do you think?

Woman.   I think, they just can't think of anything else to do. Would this count as conservative?

Man.   OK. When you ride these bulls now, you can try to do it in an entirely new way. I think, what you are talking about is a good thing, after all. It's like taking a used sheet of paper and writing on its clean side.

Heim.   It's definitely better, than taking a whole clean sheet. That would be a waste.

Woman.   But don't you think that if you are writing on a clean side of a used sheet, you'll come up with something other, than what it would be, if you'd take a whole clean sheet?

Man.   Rubbish. You gotta know, what you want to put on paper, before you start scribbling, in any case. And if you do it, it doesn't matter what you scribble on.

Woman.   Where are those wretched bulls, anyway?

Heim.   There are three. Choose one.

Woman.   I'll take the biggest one. It must be the strongest one.

Man.   Why are the biggest animals always chosen more, I wonder?

Woman.   Because bigger means stronger and, therefore, better equipped for finding food.

Man.   In lions' prides it's lionesses who do most hunting, but they are smaller, than lions. Why?

Woman.   I don't know. Where are those damned bulls?

Heim.   Just before you. Pick up one and ride. See what you can talk it into.

Woman.   What should I be aiming at? Is it to stay on its back for as long, as possible, or to make it angry and play torero?

Man.   These two things sometimes get confused, you know. See how you go. Whatever you enjoy more.

Woman comes close to one of the bulls and climbs on its back. She pats it on the neck with a whip and then whips harder.

Woman.   Go! Allez!

The bull starts shaking its neck and back, trying to get rid of Woman.

Heim.   Say something nice, or he'll squash you in a second!
Woman.   What? I'm too shaken to think of anything! Ah! Got it! Let's compromise!
Man.   Since he's too busy running, I'll be speaking for him. As an official representative. Did you mean com-promise, like you know, promise two convergent things?
Woman.   I haven't thought about it, but, yeah, something like this. What's promising convergent things is anyway?
Man.   You'll see. Try one, go ahead.
Woman.   Er . . . What can it be that'll make him feel better . . . I have no idea, actually. I promise, I will try and be fair to you.
Man.   I'll be fair, too. Let's start now. Come on, it's my, pardon me, his turn to ride on your back.
Woman.   Why? What do you mean?
Man.   This must be fair. If you ride on his back, he must be able to ride on yours.
Woman.   But it's impossible. And I don't want to, anyway. And I cannot gallop, either.
Man.   You don't have to gallop. There is another way to run. You know, first your front legs make a step, then your back ones do. Or your hands and feet do, it's the same thing. I've forgotten, what it's called, but it's the idea which is important. Best horses run this way.

Woman.	It's counter-evolutionary. First hands, then feet. Besides, it was Europe who rode on bull Zeus' back, not him on hers.
Heim.	Everything that has something to do with Europe, is so passé. We live a new kind of life in a new kind of society in a new world.
Woman.	Can't you take out some of these 'new'? There are way too many. It makes me feel, like I knew something, but forgotten, what it was. Is his name Zeus, by the way?
Man.	Try to remember.
Woman.	Er . . . He can't ride on my back, because he's much too heavy!
Man.	You could put on weight for your new role. Eat a bread roll everyday and you'll be there in no time!
Heim.	You can take up a job in the bakery. You'll have a couple of rolls everyday and soon you'll be able to fill in your new role. I mean, carrying Zeus on your back.
Woman.	So how many roles will it be altogether? Three?
Man.	You got confused, counting. Two rolls and one role. You can't add them up, because they are all different, it's not the same kind of thing.
Woman.	Then why do they all come together? I mean, roles and rolls?
Heim.	Everything must have a proper material basis. With a proper material basis, all animals are equal.
Woman.	But some are more equal, than others, as we all know. Does a proper material basis mean, that you've got to eat enough bread rolls to become fat enough to carry a bull?
Heim.	What would you think, it means? Suggest an alternative.
Woman.	Wouldn't it be easier, if Zeus lost some weight? For me, at least. And it's also more economical. And fair.

Man.	Done. This bull is going to be on a strict calorie-controlled diet from now on. If you think it will make your carrying role easier . . .
Woman.	My caring role? Of course, it would. If he won't eat as much, it would be splendid.
Man.	I said carrying, not caring.
Woman.	Yes, I see, it's different. Just before we move on, I want to say something. If people didn't consume so much, maybe the whole equality problem would look different. And carrying, too. I mean caring. Anyway, what the other two bulls are like?
Heim.	Have a look. You may want to try a different approach now. Not so straightforward, you know.
Woman.	I'll keep it for the cow. You've got one, haven't you? By the way, she can't be as heavy, as Zeus, can she? How many pounds does she weigh?
Heim.	Do you want to start with her?
Woman.	Mm . . . I'm not sure. Maybe, I should exhaust other possibilities first. Or would that be fostering negative stereotypes? Anyway, it's better to foster stereotypes, than children, wouldn't you agree? If you have some choice left, of course.
Heim.	You must feel free. Everything is allowed now.
Woman.	Really? It makes it boring. There must be left something forbidden or, at least, disapproved of. You know, just to add some emotion. It's mostly uncertainty and disapproval of others that do it.
Heim.	To add emotion to what?
Woman.	Er . . . To all kinds of experiences.
Man.	You are too rational. You speak, as if you were mixing a sauce for a roast. And I definitely disapprove of it. Does it add emotion to your experience?
Woman.	Not really. Something must be wrong in this equation. Anyway, what's the worst thing I could try? Bigamy?

	What would this amount to, in terms of riding these bulls?
Heim.	A corrida with two bulls at once? Isn't it too dangerous? It's unheard of.
Woman.	It will prove, that I am no worse than a regular torero. On the contrary, it will make me twice as good.
Man.	Very well. Go ahead, do it. These two animals are at your disposal.
Woman.	And a cow?
Heim.	Yeah, sure. Do you want to involve her, too?
Woman.	I'll start with the bulls. How can I make them both interested, do you have ideas?
Heim.	You sure know.
Woman.	(speaking to one of the bulls). You are better, than your other mate over there.

The bull starts stamping its hooves on the ground with force.

Man.	Good. See. It works. Go on.
Woman.	(speaking to another bull). You are better, than the other bull.

The second bull starts jumping.

| Woman. | I am disappointed in both of them. It seems, that a guaranteed way to make any of them interested, is a bit of simple flattery. Or making them jealous, which is nearly the same thing,—one gets jealous, when the other one is being flattered. It's too simple. |

Heim and Man (together). You are manipulative. And dishonest!

| Heim. | Besides, if any of them will understand that, they'll change their mind. |

Woman.   Change their mind about what? Does it ever happen? Besides, does it come from the inside of their mind, what's happening now?

Man.   You are as hard as nails.

Woman.   Polished.

Heim.   Don't you feel, you are loosing something by all this calculating? By being too rational? What is it, you'd really like them to be? Apart from being interested in you?

Woman.   I'd say, it's enough, if it's true. Or nearly so. Of course, there is something else I need.

Man and Heim (together). What? What is it? Tell us now!

Woman.   Don't you know? Try to guess. Let's see, whose guess is going to be best.

Man.   You need understanding and support.

Woman.   It's questionable, if you can actually understand another person. Especially, if you are really tied to them. And support is such a condescending word.

Heim.   Condescending?

Woman.   Yeah. I mean, if you expect somebody to cook all your meals, twice a day, morning and night, every day, who is supporting whom?

Man.   It can be mutual. You expect something like this too.

Woman.   Not any more. Well-adjusted women are self-sufficient these days.

Heim.   The word 'self-sufficient' makes me thing of a cow milking itself. This is self-sufficiency indeed, is it not?

Woman.   OK. It's your turn now. What, do you think, I may want?

Heim.   You want . . . You want somebody to fulfil all your needs, whatever they might be, and love you.

Woman.   What needs? And what do you mean by love me?

Heim.   Just any needs, whatever. It can be money, or just a good time. And by love I mean that you want somebody to think you are the best.

Woman. Do you, really, think so?

Heim. At the moment, I'm focused on what it is, you could need.

Woman. In this case, the best person, obviously, is the one, who needs less. A perfect woman is the one, who doesn't need anything at all. At least, it's not as tiring.

Man. This sounds close to true.

Heim. It's too simple, again. There is more to relationships, than self-sufficiency.

Woman. What's a relationship? I'm not sure, I know what it is, but I hate the word. I mean, there is marriage and there is free love, but what's a relationship?

Man. It's when you mix these two in a certain proportion, you get a relationship.

Woman. What proportion?

Heim. You can take both in a different proportion each time. Then it'll be always different, and not that simple.

Woman. Speaking of simple. Do you think, we can check any of this on the animals?

Man. Check what?

Woman. The self-sufficiency theory. I am sure, if the cow is fed grass from her own little patch, the bull will love her more, than when they all are fed together, off the same lawn.

Heim. Start fencing a little separate paddock for each of them, and we'll see what happens. In the meantime, think about how you are going to construct your relationship with the cow. She is in the game too, remember.

Woman. I don't have to tell you, what I want to do with the cow, do I? I am not going to ride her, this would be against female sisterhood.

Heim. Why? On the contrary, sisterhood requires, that there'd be no difference between a cow and a bull. So you must ride both, to prove that.

Woman.   Why does sisterhood require it? I can't see a connection.

Heim.   The real connection happens, when bulls and cows run neck to neck. If you can organize this, it shows your ultimate love for your sisters.

Woman.   Why? I don't want to organize anything like this. And she is not my sister. She is an ugly cow. If I ride her, it'll make her slower. If she runs neck to neck with some bulls, on the other hand, it may wear her out.

Heim.   These are all sapphisms, I mean, sophisms. We got distracted. Remember, we've got to fence out these three animals, two bulls and a cow, and see whether it will affect their love positively, or negatively.

Woman.   Let's do it now.

Man, Woman and Heim pick up a few fences and start moving them. As they do so, Vania Juan appears on the stage.

Vania Juan. Hello, my name is Juan. I'm Spanish. You can call me Vania, if it's easier for you. What are you doing?

Heim.   We actually have a corrida here. A jumbo corrida, I could say. We have three bulls and a cow. And the three of us—Man here, Woman and myself—are acting as toreros. We play it in our own special way, however. Anyone can pick up as many animals, as they want, to play with. Would you like to join?

Vania Juan. What? I'm not sure I've heard correctly. You are having corrida with a cattle herd? It can't be. Corrida is exclusive. One torero, one bull.

Woman and Man (together). If you can't hear, we can easily organize a translator for you. And why does it have to be exclusive? Everything is inclusive these days. Which means, it's not a herd, it's two carefully selected teams.

Vania Juan. What teams?

Heim.   A team of bulls and a team of toreros.

Woman.	You've forgotten the cow. She is on the team, too.
Man.	Which team?
Woman.	The team of bulls, obviously.
Man.	It's a contradiction in terms. A cow cannot be on the team of bulls. Because she is not a bull. Think it over.
Heim.	Listen, I have. TEAM-TAM. Does it sound good? The great sponsor of the corrida show you are watching, is TEAM-TAM Ltd.
Vania-Juan.	What's TEAM—TAM? What do you mean?
Heim.	It's a kind of chocolate biscuits. Some people think they are better, than other kinds.
Vania-Juan.	I don't like it at all. This is . . . what do you call it? Kitsch.
Heim.	You may not like it, but this is not, what kitsch means. Kitsch means mass-produced and in vulgar popular taste.
Vania-Juan.	Doesn't matter. We call this kitsch in Spain. Kitschos.
Heim.	I see. This corrida may be kitshchos, but, at least, it is not as machos as some other are. It's explorative in spirit. Do you want to stay, Juan, and see what happens next? When every animal has its own little paddock to eat grass off?

Vania-Juan hesitates for a few seconds and then nods an agreement.

ACT 3.

Vania Juan walks along the edge of the arena until he comes close to the three bulls.

Vania-Juan.	I am going to show you now, how it has to be done.
Heim.	Has anybody ever shown to you, how it has to be done?

163

Vania-Juan. Actually, no. But I think I know it, anyway.

Heim.   How?

Vania-Juan. It's instinctive, in my blood.

Woman.   Which one of these bulls are you going to fight with?

Vania-Juan. I'll try them all, and the one, who gets most angry, will be a good rival for me.

Vania-Juan pokes each of the three bulls with his knife. Two of the bulls step back and start walking away from him. The one that's left, makes a sound and lowers his head and takes a threatening position with his horns facing up.

Vania-Juan. See, this one is a real fighter. I'll be playing with him.

Woman.   Hasn't he got even the least bit of common sense? Doesn't he know, he is going to die?

Vania-Juan. How should he know?

Woman.   But the other two bulls do. I don't know, how. Perhaps, because they can see a knife in your hand.

Vania-Juan. He is a hero. A real male.

Woman.   It is instinctive.

Vania-Juan. I think so.

Woman.   The other two have an instinct of self-preservation, and it's more important to them. And this one wants to fight. Why?

Man.   They are like a different species.

Heim.   The one that wants to fight is a born leader. The other two, who want to save their lives, are born followers. They are made of another kind of dough, the crowd material.

Woman.   Do you think, something can be done, to turn the other two into fighters? I mean, it might depend on circumstances, as well as the nature, right?

Heim. Let's try and make the other two wanting to fight. How can it be done? Do you think, to cheer them up, we should call them bull fighters?

Man. Fighter bulls, not bull fighters. What difference does it make what do we call them?

Heim. It may have some. I mean, if you want to make somebody to take risks, it does matter, what you call them. Alternatively, you can call them crazy bully bulls. But I think, it will have a pacifying, rather than an invigorating, effect on them.

Woman. We can call them bull leaders, bleaders, for short.

Vania-Juan. Stop it. I think I will first do this one, and then we'll see.

Heim. After you've killed this one, the other two may change their opinion on how much they want to fight. It's only natural.

Woman. Let's divide them. We'll try to involve one of these two into fighting, before the leader is killed, and the other one—maybe after that?

Man. Good. Which one are we going to take now?

Heim. The one, that looks like he wants to do it too, when you start playing with their leader.

Woman. They both don't look like it.

Vania-Juan bares his knife and lunges before the leader bull. The leader bull makes a jump and lowers his head again. The other two bulls step further away.

Woman. It doesn't look, like they feel any affinity with this one. If you want to make them fight, it should be something, that involves them personally.

Man. Like what?

Woman. We can pull their tails again, of course, but we've done it before. Let's try something different. For example,

165

	if you say something really offensive, it may help turn their peaceful mood into something more adequate.
Man.	Is it how great leaders are born?
Heim.	Or maybe, great bullies. It's not the same thing, you know.
Man.	Great leaders attack first, they don't just respond to offences. This is what makes them great.
Woman.	Who do they attack?
Vania-Juan.	Enough theorizing. It is so kitsch. Let's start now. I know what to do, to get the other two bulls involved, too.